THE FABULOUS FIFTY

Books by Morton Grosser

Diesel: The Man and the Engine (nonfiction)
The Snake Horn
The Fabulous Fifty

THE
FABULOUS FIFTY

☆ ☆ ☆ ☆ ☆

Morton Grosser

A JEAN KARL BOOK

ATHENEUM 1990 NEW YORK

Collier Macmillan Canada
Toronto
Maxwell Macmillan International Publishing Group
New York • Oxford • Singapore • Sydney

Atheneum
Macmillan Publishing Company
866 Third Avenue
New York, NY 10022

Collier Macmillan Canada, Inc.
1200 Eglinton Avenue East
Suite 200
Don Mills, Ontario M3C 3N1

First Edition
Designed by Nancy B. Williams
Printed in the United States of America
10   9   8   7   6   5   4   3   2   1

Library of Congress Cataloging-in-Publication Data

Grosser, Morton.
The Fabulous Fifty/Morton Grosser—1st ed.
p.   cm.
"A Jean Karl book."
Summary: In the summer of 1921, fourteen-year-old Sol seeks independence from his family and his South Philadelphia neighborhood and joins his pals in their obsessive scheme to get to the World Series by clipping newspaper coupons.
[1. Baseball—Fiction. 2. Philadelphia (Pa.)—Fiction.]
I. Title.
PZ7.G907Fab   1990   [Fic]—dc20   89-77999   CIP   AC
ISBN 0-689-31656-9

This novel is a work of fiction. The Fabulous Fifty contest actually occurred, but other references to historical events, to real people living or dead, or to real locales are intended only to give the work a setting in historical reality. Other names, characters, places, and incidents are the product of the author's imagination.

*This book is dedicated
to my father,
Albert J. Grosser,
and my son,
Adam Grosser*

CHAPTER 1

Tony Ammanati was the first technical businessman I ever knew. He stole the magnetos and spark coils from Model T Fords and built them into transmitters for radio amateurs. Tony was small and wiry, a wise guy, a fast runner, and my best friend. He was good at business: He had low overhead, free materials, and a good product with an unbeatable price. I worked with him for three years, sometimes in manufacturing and sometimes in procurement.

We did what we had to. In 1921, when we were both 15, money was hard to get. We lived on South Street, a Philadelphia melting pot like you used to see pictures of in articles about the Statue of Liberty. The sidewalks were crowded with old ladies in kerchiefs talking Russian and Italian and Yiddish, and the street was full of pushcart men selling everything from old clothes to water ice.

In the summer you could buy two hot buttered ears of Jersey corn for a penny, and if you were quick you could grab a pickle from the barrel when the pushcart man turned to put the penny in his purse. *"Dirty kids! Crooks! Get outa here, little crooks!"* After you ran through a couple of alleys you could sit on the curb and swap bites of the wonderful sweet corn and the cold tart pickle. I loved summer, even the hot, sticky nights when we brought our mattresses out on the roof to get a little air. There was no school, there was all-day stickball, and there were fire hydrants to open on the real scorchers. It was a lot better than the winters.

Philadelphia winters were dank months of icy mornings and scratchy wool sweaters. The winter of 1921 seemed endless. The gutters were full of soot-colored snow in March, and everyone's house smelled of boiled cabbage. We couldn't wait for the baseball season to start and for the girls to start wearing thin cotton dresses again. One Saturday morning Tony and I were sitting on Old Man Casati's steps trying to decide if Mark Kolaks was lying when he said that Cissie Nolan didn't wear underwear. The steps were still damp from being washed and the cold stone came right through my corduroy knickers. I could feel my bottom slowly going numb. Tony picked up Casati's morning *Clarion* and turned through it. Suddenly he stopped and held open a double page full of stars and rockets. "Look at this!" Across the top was a headline as big as the one for the Armistice: THE FABULOUS FIFTY—MAMMOTH PRIZES FOR 50 LUCKY READERS OF PHILADELPHIA'S LEADING DAILY!

We read the page spellbound. The *Clarion* was sponsoring the biggest contest in the history of Philadelphia. The fifty winners were going to be taken to the 1921 World Series on a special train. They would stay at America's most splendid and luxurious hostelries and they would be wined and dined and receive many valuable prizes, all courtesy of the *Clarion* and all absolutely free. There was a drawing of a fancy couple getting on the train with reporters taking their pictures.

"Wow," Tony said, "Let's see what you have to do to win." MERELY ENTER THIS SIMPLE CONTEST! It looked simple too—no trick puzzle pictures or secret words to unscramble. Beginning that day, March 5, the *Clarion* would print a coupon in the paper every day. You just cut the coupons out, and on August 15 you sent them to the paper. The fifty people who sent in the most coupons were the winners. Like they said, it was simple.

"That's what you think," Tony said. "This is gonna be tough." He pointed to the fine print at the bottom of the page. First, the daily coupons were just bait—chicken feed. Every day the *Clarion* would issue some unmarked "Lucky Bonus Papers" with a whole page of coupons in them, and each new subscription to the paper was worth 200 coupons. But the real catch was one we both understood as soon as Tony mentioned it: Every crook in the city would be working on angles to win the contest. That's the way it was in Philadelphia.

We read the rules three or four times. I looked at the drawing of the winners and thought about how famous they would be. I imagined my picture in the paper, standing between my parents in front of our store. Tony poked me in the ribs. "We gotta enter."

"You're crazy. We wouldn't have a chance."

"Not just us—the whole club."

"You're out of your Egyptian mind." My older sister, Elena, said that a lot.

Tony looked surprised. "I'm the president."

"Well, I'm the vice president. We gotta have a vote."

"Okay, we'll have a meeting tonight and vote."

"I think you're nuts."

Tony took out his stag-handled jackknife and slit coupon number one out of Old Man Casati's *Clarion*. "We'll see who's nuts, you dumb Greek."

CHAPTER 2

My name is Solon Demetrios Janus. That may sound like a mouthful, but on a street where people were named Wisnievics or Tagliarelli, Sol Janus was practically shorthand. It was almost too short to be comfortable. It wasn't smart to stick out on South Street unless you were a politician, and we already stuck out because my father was the only Greek in Philadelphia who had a hardware store. My nearest approach to politics was being vice president of our club.

We met that night in the kitchen behind Mrs. Goodman's candy store on Reese Street. Mrs. Goodman was a widow with a bun of wiry gray hair, and her son, Harry, was in the club. That was unusual because kids on South Street mostly stayed with their own kind. We had the only mixed club: One Italian, one Greek, one Irishman, one Pole, and one Jew. It sounds like National Brotherhood Week now, but in 1921 that wasn't in. Mrs. Goodman was proud of Harry, but she loved Tony because he was so little; she would give him these big hugs like he was going to disappear into her dress.

Before the meeting Tony bought us a nickel's worth of potato chips, a big, greasy paper bag filled from the giant can that Mrs. Goodman made fresh every day. It was a bribe I could never resist. He called the meeting to order by knocking on the kitchen table with a salt shaker. "All right, everybody, this is a very important meeting."

"What's the big deal?" Mark Kolaks asked.

Tony unfolded the Fabulous Fifty announcement from the *Clarion* and spread it across the table. "Take a look at that. Everything is *free.*" He looked at Bobby Kelly. Bobby's father was a bricklayer, and Bobby had nine brothers and sisters. He had never had a new toy or piece of clothing in his life. "Free," Tony repeated. "All we have to do is collect enough coupons."

Bobby was a slow reader, and we waited while he finished the page. "Well, there has to be a catch to it."

"More than one," Tony agreed. What a politician, I thought.

"You're right, Bob," I said, jumping on the bandwagon. I was skeptical about the plan too, and I wanted to stay on Bobby's good side because he was Cissie Nolan's cousin. I dreamed about Cissie every night. She had red hair and creamy white skin and a freckled turned-up nose that you would never see on a Greek girl. She had freckles on her shoulders too, and I wondered how far down they went.

"What do you think, Sol?" Harry asked me for the second time.

I ate a potato chip to cover up. "About what?"

"About the contest, stupid," Tony said.

"I'm not sure we can do it."

"You know every crook in town is gonna be in there," Mark said.

"Right," Tony said. "So we gotta cheat better than them."

"More efficiently," I said.

"You got any ideas to go with the big words?"

I took a swing at him, and he ducked and laughed. "Well, we can start like you did this morning. We can cut the coupons out of everyone's papers before they get them."

"That ain't hard," Mark said. "Hymie Silverstein delivers the papers on South and Lombard—"

"Hymie!" Tony broke in. "He can barely carry his violin case."

"Well, maybe so, but he's doing it. My cousin Joe drives the paper truck. I can get the route from him."

"We'll have to take turns tailing him," I said.

"You mean we have to get up earlier than for school?" Harry groaned through a mouthful of potato chips.

"Shut up, fatso," Tony said. "You'll take turns like everybody. But we have to think of more angles."

Bobby sat quietly, looking worried. "Look," he said to Tony, "Suppose we get all these coupons and everything and win the contest. Who goes on the trip and gets the prizes?"

Tony looked as though his honor had been questioned. "Well, we choose out, and the guy who wins goes."

"You mean one potato, two potato?" Bobby looked appalled.

"Or we'll pull straws or something," Tony said, less sure.

"So what do the rest of us get for all the work?" Mark asked. There was an awkward silence. Tony read through the announcement again. "Look, it says here, hundreds of prizes including Stetson hats, Kodak cameras, Parker pens, and many others to be announced. How about if the guy who wins goes to the Series but he don't get any of the prizes. We split them up between us. That way everybody gets something."

Bobby thought about it. "Well," he said hesitantly, "if we all really get something . . ."

"Think about if we win it," Tony said. "It ain't just the prizes. We'll be famous. Everybody in Philly will know that we did it."

I thought about Cissie knowing that I did it.

"As long as we all get something," Bobby said.

"It's okay with me," Mark said.

"I'm not getting up early the first day," Harry said.

Tony looked at me. "I still think it's a long shot, but if everybody else wants to I guess I'm in too."

"Sol the Greek!" Tony crowed. "You're first!"

We decided that I would start collecting coupons Monday morning. On Sunday Mark's cousin drew us a map of Hymie Silverstein's route, and Sunday night I sharpened my Schrade pocketknife on my father's oilstone and finished the edges on the razor strop beside his workbench. Both blades shaved the hair on my arm easily. My mother usually woke me up for school, but that night I jerked awake every few minutes so I wouldn't oversleep. At four-thirty I slipped out of bed and pulled on my underwear and clammy knickers in the dark. My brother, Georgios, muttered in his sleep when I tiptoed past his bed. I crept downstairs in my socks, holding my breath at every creaky step, put on my shoes, and eased the front door shut behind me. The sky was gray and cold and the street was deserted. I walked to the end of the block and stood against a wall, waiting for Hymie. I was shivering by the time he came around the corner with two bags of *Clarions* slung over his scrawny shoulders.

The gray light was good for tailing. I followed the route two blocks behind Hymie, ducking behind a step or into a doorway when he looked back. By the tenth house I had a smooth routine: Check the street in both directions, open Hymie's carefully folded *Clarion,* slit the coupon out of the first page, refold the paper. I followed Hymie down South Street to Swanson, along Swanson to Bainbridge, up Bainbridge to Eighth, across Eighth to Lombard, and down Lombard to Swanson again.

People got up early in 1921. I missed a dozen papers that women came out to get before breakfast, and three more because a milkman turned onto Bainbridge behind me. When I counted the coupons in my bedroom, I had 121. I went off to school feeling smug.

"Not bad," Tony said, when I told the club in the schoolyard.

"Whatdya mean, not bad? I thought it was pretty good."

"A hundred and twenty-one sounds pretty good to me," Harry said.

"I figured it out," I said. "If you clipped one coupon every day you'd have a hundred sixty-four for the whole contest. If we keep on like this we'll have nineteen thousand."

"We're gonna have to do a hell of a lot better than that to win."

"How do you know?"

"I just know. Wait and see."

"Well, what else can we do?" Mark asked. The school bell rang and Tony looked up at the doorway of the Foote School thoughtfully. "I don't know yet. We'll talk about it later."

CHAPTER 3

By March 15 I knew Tony was right. At first it looked easy; we clipped the coupons from Hymie's route for a week without getting caught. We were doing better every day— "More efficient," Harry said when he brought in 140 coupons on Friday the eleventh. The weekend was harder because people got up at different times and fewer families took the Sunday *Clarion*. Saturday morning we did the Orthodox Jews, because they couldn't pick up their papers till sunset. Even so we only got a measly sixty-three coupons for the whole weekend.

Tony decided to switch days with me the week of the fourteenth, and on Monday he broke our record with 152 coupons. We had collected 874 coupons in the first nine days and all of us except Tony thought we were home free. We figured we could keep clipping Hymie's coupons right up to the end of the contest.

When I started out Tuesday morning, I felt like a professional. I slid along two blocks behind Hymie, determined to beat Tony's record. I guessed that he had detoured to clip part of another route and cut back to finish Hymie's. I tried that on Kater Street, moving fast, and got eighteen extra coupons. Hot stuff, I thought, and backtracked to pick up Hymie on Bainbridge. At the last house I bent down to unfold the paper and a woman in a black dress jumped out of a doorway and grabbed me—she must have been waiting. She clutched the front of my jacket and pulled me up against her. "Crook," she whispered fiercely in my face. Her breath had garlic on it at six o'clock in the morning. "I'll fix you." I was so close I could see the hairs in the mole on her upper lip. She raised her arm and I saw that she had a rolling pin in her other hand. I had never fought a woman in my life, but when she started to swing I reached up and grabbed her wrist without thinking. The rolling pin stopped in midair. We were both amazed. I held her arm motionless and the realization that I was stronger than she was flowed over me. Don't laugh, I told myself, but it was no use; a helpless grin of triumph spread over my face like a blush. "Crook, little crook," she said through clenched teeth, and two tears squeezed out of her eyes and ran down her cheeks. I tensed to run, and she spat all over my face. I jerked my jacket out of her hand and then took off and heard the rolling pin hit the street behind me.

Get out of there. I was running down Swanson Street, wiping spit off my face with my sleeve, when I noticed that Hymie was nowhere in sight ahead of me. That's funny, I thought, the old woman only took a few seconds. Then I noticed that there were no papers at his regular houses. Maybe the delivery truck shorted him. It was turning out to be a peculiar day. I walked back along the route slowly, and as I came to Swanson's Alley something warned me to stop. I eased up to the corner and peeked around it. The hairs on the back of my neck went up. Two guys in dark suits were standing in the alley. One of them was holding a big switchblade, and the other one was holding Hymie

Silverstein against the wall like a corduroy-knickered string bean. Hymie was shaking with fright. "Where are they?" the guy with the knife asked.

"I don't know," Hymie said, "honest." The guy tossed the knife up and caught it. *"La verita pura,"* he said to the other one with a little smile. It didn't take any brains to figure out: Hymie's Italian customers had wondered where their coupons were going and called in some muscle. The obvious suspect was Hymie.

"Listen, sheenie." The knife guy drew a little circle around Hymie's fly with the point of the switchblade. "Maybe they didn't shorten it enough the first time. Maybe we oughta do it again." Hymie started to cry and a dark blotch spread across the front of his pants. "I told you I don't know," he pleaded. "I just deliver the papers." He began to cry uncontrollably and the one holding him lifted him up and knocked his head against the wall a little: "Cut it out." Hymie couldn't stop; the guy slapped him, and he vomited all over the dark suit. The hit man swatted at his lapels furiously. "You Jew son of a bitch, I'll fix you for that!"

You might be thinking that I was going to be a hero, huh? Run in there like a South Street Zorro with my razor-sharp Schrade coupon clipper and save Hymie Silverstein. You'd be out of your Egyptian mind. I knew I had to distract them though, because if they cut up Hymie he'd lose the route, they'd put one of their own kids on it, and that would be the end of our coupons. I backed away from the corner, trying to think of something.

There was a basket of coal clinkers at the curb—that was it. I grabbed a handful of clinkers and picked up two empty milk bottles from the steps of the nearest house. When I peered around the corner the knife point was just grazing Hymie's face and the guy looked serious. Hymie looked like a wax doll. There was a light on in the kitchen of the third house in the alley. I threw the clinkers hard at the window with my right hand and then lofted the milk bottles down the alley underhand with my left. My gym teacher would have been proud. The people in the kitchen heard a bunch of rocks hit their window and a crash of broken glass. In a second the window was up and a furious woman was looking into the alley. "You!" She pointed at the Italians and shot a stream of Russian over her shoulder.

The noise that came from behind her sounded like a wounded bear. The back door of the house slammed open and a huge bearded man burst into the alley clutching a meat cleaver. He was the size of a bear and his eyes were popping out of their sockets with rage. "Wop!" he roared, and went straight for the two Italians. The guy with the knife turned and ran for his life. The other one dropped Hymie, who had fainted. Hymie fell forward, the guy tripped over him, and as he tried to get up the Russian brought his boot down on the guy's ankle like a pile driver. I could hear the bones breaking thirty feet away. The Italian screamed but—*miracolo!*—he struggled to his feet and started to run anyway, limping and hopping down the alley. The Russian started after him with the cleaver, and his wife yelled at him from the kitchen. He stopped, and then he noticed Hymie lying in the alley in a pool of vomit. "*Oy,*" the Russian said. He knelt down and felt Hymie's face. The wife came out and said something in Russian, and the man handed her the cleaver, picked up Hymie like a rag doll, and carried him into the house. By that time there were a dozen people in the alley, shouting to their relatives and pointing at the upstairs windows, trying to figure out which one was broken. I beat it, walking at first, then running as fast as I could.

CHAPTER 4

Tony was plenty disappointed at the meeting that night. "You only got sixty-eight? I'm tellin' you guys, you gotta pick it up or we're gonna lose." When I explained why I only had sixty-eight he turned prickly. "It ain't the Italians' fault. They only need the Mafia because everybody picks on them." He didn't say it was the Greeks' fault or the Jews' fault, but you could tell that was what he was thinking. "We gotta get some more angles," he said, looking at me.

"We could try another route. I got eighteen from Kater Street."

"It's too close. The Mafia's gonna be watching everything around here now."

"What about the bonus papers?"

"I give up, what about them?"

"Has Hymie delivered any?"

Tony shrugged. "If he has, nobody's talkin' about it."

"I heard that a guy up on Arch Street got one," Mark said. "It had a hundred coupons in it."

"A hundred coupons!" Harry whistled. "Boy, we should get some of them."

"Fat chance," Bobby said. "They probably guard them like money." He was beginning to lose what confidence we had pumped into him.

"Maybe," Mark said. "But somebody has to put them in the papers."

"Probably the cops," Bobby said.

I thought about that. "No, they have to do it at the *Clarion*. They have to know how many they print and how many they put on each route so there's a uniform distribution." That was from my math lessons with Mr. Feuter.

Tony kicked the leg of Mrs. Goodman's table. "Dammit, Janus, all you got is big words and little ideas."

"Watch the table," Harry said.

"Don't blame me for those hoods," I said. "I don't see any bonus papers from your route."

"I got more coupons than you."

"For now. I'll pass you."

"I could ask my cousin Joe," Mark said.

"Sixty-eight lousy coupons! You couldn't pass me if I was on crutches."

"Keep it up and you will be."

"Cut it out," Harry said, and tossed me a potato chip.

"Maybe he could find out how they work the bonus papers," Mark said.

Tony shook his head. "If your cousin knows, then everybody at the paper knows, and they'd get the bonus papers."

"But nobody who works for the *Clarion* can enter the contest."

"They got relatives, don't they?"

I finally had an idea. "Look, there's only two ways they can send out bonus coupons. They can print them in special papers, or they can print them on separate pages and stick a page into a few papers a day. That's easier but it's a lot riskier because they know people will steal the coupon pages."

Bobby nodded. "That sounds right."

"So what?"

"So they probably print them right in. And if they do, they have to know which papers have them, so there has to be a mark or a code on the front of the bonus paper someplace."

"Wow," Harry said.

"We need to know which system they use, and that's something Joe could probably find out."

"And then what?" Tony asked.

"If we can find out I'll tell you what."

"Okay, I'll ask," Mark said. "But where do we get coupons in the meantime?"

"We have to work other routes until they get wise to us," Tony said.

When we started spreading out, we really appreciated Hymie. During the next two weeks we went farther away every morning. Tony and I were both late to school on our collecting days. We averaged about 110 coupons a day— not enough, Tony kept saying—and one day Harry tried a route near Ninth and Christian where the papers were already clipped. People were learning fast.

Mark's cousin tried to find out about the bonus papers, but it was the best-kept secret at the *Clarion.* They were controlled by the publisher's brother, who claimed that each district got the same number of coupons. "Sure they do," Tony said at our next meeting. "Find out where the publisher's brother's family lives, and that's where the bonus papers will be."

I decided to try Hymie's route again the next Monday. I

thought that maybe the Mafia had simmered down by then. I waited for Hymie at my usual starting point, but when he came around the corner there were two surprises. First, he didn't have any *Clarion* bags over his shoulders. Second, he wasn't alone. The papers were carried by a huge companion who looked like a younger and slightly smaller edition of the Russian bear. He wore the bags of newspapers like feather pillows and he kept one giant paw on Hymie's shoulder as they walked along. Hymie had been adopted.

I can handle that, I thought. I let them get a block ahead of me, and just as I was ready to start clipping, two more men turned the corner. I recognized one: It was Angelo Morello, Tony's cousin who had quit high school last year. He had grown a wispy mustache and wore a cheap version of the pin-striped suit. The other guy was a scrawny cutout of Morello; his suit looked like it was made of cardboard. They trailed along behind Hymie and his friend, watching for monkey business. Every few minutes the big Russian turned and scowled at them.

So the Mafia had set up a patrol to keep Hymie from clipping the papers! I was thrilled. I slid in two blocks behind the train and picked up 153 coupons.

"Oh boy, I love it." Harry grinned when I told the story.

"Yeah, that's good," Tony said. I knew he would try to get his record back, but the next morning he was ambushed by the same woman that grabbed me on Bainbridge Street. This time she yelled for the cops, and Tony had his face scratched up and a bag of eggshells and coffee grounds emptied on his head. He got away by the skin of his teeth and came home with sixty-five coupons. When he told us about it, I just looked at him.

Bobby had only been averaging about a hundred coupons, but on Thursday of that week he came to school with a smile on his face. When we met in the yard to find out how many he had, he said, "Guess."

"A hundred and forty?"

"Nope."

"More or less?" Tony asked impatiently.

"More."

"A hundred and sixty?" That would be a new record.

"More."

"More? C'mon, we give up."

"Two hundred and seventeen."

Mark whistled. "Two seventeen! You really mean it?"

Bobby lowered his voice to a whisper. "I got a bonus paper."

We pounded him on the back and yelled like he had hit a homer with the bags full. Everyone in the school yard looked over to see what was happening. "Shut up, jerks," Tony ordered. "Where'd you find it?"

"On Lombard. I unfolded the paper to clip the coupon and the back half fell out. When I put it back, I saw that it had a page that was all coupons, so I took the whole paper."

"Good job," I said. Just then we heard a loud cheer from the other side of the school yard. It was a bunch of eighth-grade girls. They were looking over at us, watching for our reaction. "Maybe they got a bonus paper too," Harry said.

"Shut up," Tony said.

"But maybe they're collecting coupons too. If they got a bonus—"

"Goodman, if you mention the damn bonus paper one more time I'm gonna suspend you. We don't want anybody to know about it, understand?"

"Yeah, but—"

"Don't but me. Janus, find out what they're cheering about."

"Me? Why me?"

"Look over there."

I hadn't even noticed who the girls were. When I looked again they were all grinning at us, and I realized that the closest one was Cissie Nolan.

Tony dug me in the ribs. "That's why, lover boy. We need some news from your girlfriend. We know one thing about her already, right?"

A wave of rage swept over me and I swung on Tony with all my might. I never even saw him or felt my punch connect; it was like I was asleep for a second. When my vision came back he was lying on the concrete with his eyes closed, and blood was seeping from the back of his head. I was stunned. Harry knelt down beside Tony, and the other guys backed away from me in a little circle. "I'm sorry," I stammered. "I didn't mean to hurt him—I don't know what came over me." I knelt down beside Harry and tried to feel Tony's pulse like the doctor did. I couldn't feel anything. Tony didn't move. Suddenly I felt cold inside. Maybe he's dead, I thought. He couldn't be dead. I couldn't have hit him that hard.

"All right, what's the trouble here?" I looked up and saw two dark-blue suited legs in front of me. At first I thought it was the police, but it wasn't; it was Mr. Black, the principal of the Foote School.

CHAPTER 5

In eight years at the Foote School I had never spoken to the principal. I was almost more frightened to find Mr. Black standing over me than I was by Tony's unconscious body. "You boys have a fight?"

"Yes, sir, I mean no, sir, he's my best friend, I just hit him. I don't know what came over me."

"He said something about a girl," Harry volunteered. There was a noise behind me, and I realized that there was a crowd around us. "Where is he?" Miss Van Dorn, the school nurse, pushed through the circle, gave me a nasty look, and knelt down beside Tony. In a moment she had taken his pulse, sponged off the back of his head, and padded it with a bandage. She opened a bottle and held it under his nose. I caught my breath at the sharp odor and Tony's eyes flickered open. "You should be ashamed," the nurse said to me angrily. "Hitting someone smaller than yourself."

"I didn't mean to. I don't even remember hitting him."

"I bet you don't," she snapped. She picked up Tony's wrist again. "How are you feeling?" she asked him.

"Dizzy," he said. "That was some clout, greaseball."

"I'm sorry, Tony. I didn't mean it."

"I didn't know you felt that bad about her."

Miss Van Dorn stood up. "We can take him to my room and bandage his head now."

"All right, everyone, into school," Mr. Black said. The crowd melted away. I moved to follow the other kids, but Mr. Black put a hand on my shoulder. "You better come to my office, Janus." I was so scared that I started to tremble as I followed him down the hall.

I had been in the school office three times: once to deliver a note to the secretary and twice to sit on the bench when Miss Cleary gave me detention slips for drawing radio diagrams in my notebook. This time we went past the secretary into Mr. Black's private office. He pointed to a chair. "Sit there. I'll be back in a minute."

I sat down; this was big trouble. What a jerk, I thought, why did I hit him? Mr. Black seemed to be taking much longer than a minute. Maybe he was calling the police. There was an American flag in the corner and a bookcase filled with dark blue books. Over the bookcase was a framed diploma and a picture of some men and women in front of the Capitol in Washington. There was also a portrait of George Washington and a painting of Indians hunting buffalo. Three more chairs were spaced around the room, and there was a rusty baking tin under the radiator just like the one in the dining room at home.

I had thought that the principal's office would be more impressive. Mr. Black's swivel chair did have leather cushions and his desk was bigger than a teacher's, but it was the same wood, and it had a glass of yellow pencils on it instead of a pen set like the big shots' desks in the Sheaffer ads. There was a photograph of a pretty woman on the desk. I was trying to get a better look at it when Mr. Black came back. "Well, you're lucky, Janus. It looks as though Ammanati will be all right."

"I didn't mean to hurt him, honest. I told the nurse, I don't even remember hitting him."

"We have to report it anyway, that's the rule." He picked up a pencil. "How did you feel when you saw him on the ground?"

"I was surprised at first, and then I was scared. I tried to feel his pulse, but I couldn't feel anything. I was scared silly."

Mr. Black nodded and wrote something down. He looked through some papers. "Any detentions besides these two?"

"No, sir."

"You're lucky not to have been in trouble before this. You seem to be a pretty good student, Janus. You say you're a friend of Ammanati's?"

"Yes, sir, we're best friends."

He wrote some more and I noticed that his suit elbows were shiny like Mr. Feuter's. I had always thought that principals were rich. "Goodman said it was something about a girl?"

"Well, not exactly."

He leaned back in his chair. "Not exactly?"

I felt myself getting red. "It was just something Tony said."

"About a girl?"

"Yes."

He sat there looking at me, waiting.

"Look, I don't even know her, I just got excited."

"Was it an insult?"

How did he know that? "Well, sort of."

"I'd like to know who she is. I promise I won't mention it to anyone, and she won't get in trouble."

I thought about it. He did say he promised; it felt sort of grown-up.

"It was, I mean it's Cissie Nolan."

"Cissie is a very pretty girl. Very precocious. She doesn't look Greek."

"She's Irish. She's Bobby Kelly's cousin. Bobby's in our club."

"I see. And you really don't know her?"

I felt myself blushing again. "I know who she is. I haven't talked to her."

"But you hit your friend when he said something insulting about her."

"Yes, sir, but I didn't mean to hurt him. It was, it was—instinct."

Mr. Black smiled as if he couldn't help it and looked up at the ceiling. For a second I thought he might not have me arrested. "Where did you learn about instinct?"

"From Mr. Feuter. He told me about Pavlov and those dogs. But you promised about Cissie."

"That's right, I did. Don't worry, she won't get in trouble, at least on this account."

"And Mr. Feuter?"

"Mr. Feuter?"

"He won't get in trouble for teaching me about instinct instead of math?"

"You are full of surprises, Janus. No, he won't get in trouble. Now look, ordinarily I would have your father in here tomorrow, but according to the nurse your friend will be all right. If his family doesn't get upset, we'll let it ride. I am required to send a note to your parents, however. You can pick it up on the way home. I will also want you to stop in and see me from time to time."

"Yes, sir."

"And I suggest that you say hello to Cissie Nolan before you get in any more fights over her."

"Yes, sir, I will. I mean I'll try to."

"*Carpe diem*, Janus. Here's a pass to get into class."

"Thank you, sir. Carpe diem." I didn't have any idea what it meant, but I wasn't going to get arrested!

When I came out of school with Mr. Black's note in my hand the club was waiting for me. "How was it?" Tony asked.

"What?"

"You know, Black. Did he beat you up?"

"No. He was, well—he was fair."

Harry shook his head. "Boy, I wouldn't want to go in there for anything. Is he going to suspend you?"

"No. I have to take this note home to my parents."

"Uh oh," Bobby said. "I know what would happen with my old man." I had a good idea what was going to happen to me too. "Maybe you ought to drop it in a sewer," Mark said and grabbed for it. I pulled it away. "You are a dumb hero, Janus," Tony said. He wasn't even mad.

"How's your head?"

He felt the bandage. "Not bad. I'll tell my Mom I fell off the swing bar and she'll cook me some extra raviolis. I never knew those wrinkly olives made such big muscles."

"Yeah," Mark said, "you really tagged him." Everyone nodded admiringly.

"I'm still sorry."

"That's okay," Tony said. "We didn't know how it was."

"Yeah," Bobby said. "We didn't know how you felt." He patted me on the back. It almost made me forget the note.

CHAPTER 6

"From the principal?" My father's expression turned suspicious when I nodded yes. He was sitting at the dining table drinking a cup of coffee. I gave him the note and he unfolded it as if it was a letter from the president. He put on his steel-rimmed glasses and studied the message. It was only a few lines but he read it very slowly, frowning. "It's all right," I began—

"*Sopa!*" he snapped. "Speak when I say." He studied the note again. My mother came out of the kitchen. "Sol says it's all right, Pavlos." She was too late; his anger showed in the veins on his forehead as he read the note a third time. "All right? You know from who it is? From the principal! For this I'm working, so he can make a disgrace? He can work in the store!"

"Poppa, I'm sorry, it was an accident. Tony is okay, he's not even mad."

"So why the principal sends me a letter?"

"It's required. Mr. Black said they have to send a note home if anyone is hurt. But I told you, Tony is okay. It's all right, honest."

"If it's all right, they don't send a letter. A letter means you make trouble. The principal knows, soon everyone will know. The police will have your name. It will be a disgrace for the family."

"The police won't have my name, Poppa, they don't do that here."

"*Neh?* The smart man, he knows how everything works in America, but they send a letter that he makes trouble. You think I'm so dumb? *Katalaveno!*"

"Pavlos—" my mother began.

"*Sopa!*" He hit the table so hard that his coffee cup jumped out of the saucer and spilled, and I could hear the veneer crack loose from the tabletop. "Pavlos," my mother said again. "In the workshop," he said to me.

"Pavlos—" My father raised his arm and my mother pulled her apron up to her face and went into the kitchen.

I went into the workshop and stood next to the bench. "Wait," my father said. He closed the door and I heard him go upstairs and come down again. When he came back he was carrying the belt his mother had sent him from Greece. I had only seen him wear it on a few holidays. It was made of hundreds of silver wire rings braided together on thick cords of black wool. He shut the door behind him and bolted it. "There," he said, pointing to the workbench. I turned and bent over the edge of the bench. "Now," he said, "for the note from the principal," and motioned to my pants. I unbuttoned them and pulled them down. "All," he said. I pulled my underpants down, bent over the bench again, and clenched my buttocks tight. I was embarrassed. "You are sorry?"

"Yes, Poppa." For a second I thought he was going to let me off. When the belt hit the first time I gasped in spite of myself. It was ice cold and the wire rings stung like needles. I swore to myself that I wouldn't cry out. Each time the pain was worse; by the third stroke I was in agony. "You—will—not—make—a—disgrace—again!" I was holding on to the tool well at the back of the bench, trying to pinch the wood harder than he was hitting me. "Answer!"

"No, Poppa."

"Never—again!?"

"Never! God, Poppa!!" The last two strokes were so hard that I put my knuckle in my mouth to keep from shouting.

"Telos. Remember." He stepped back and motioned for me to pull up my pants. I reached down and dripped blood all over them; I had bitten my index finger almost to the bone. When I pulled up my shorts I winced; my bottom was a mass of welts and it was bleeding in places too. My father unbolted the door and it was shoved open from the other side. My mother burst into the room, her eyes blazing. *"Zoon! Barbaros!* Turk—filthy Turk!" My father shrugged and turned away. I realized that I was almost a head taller than him. My mother put her arm around me and led me into the house. I could barely walk. *"Zoon!"* she shouted over her shoulder. I was shocked; never in their angriest fights had I heard her call my father an animal. I hobbled up the stairs beside her, wincing at every step. In the bedroom she undressed me, washed and bandaged my throbbing finger, and bathed my welts gently. The Greek hero: My mother sat beside me sponging my backside while I lay there naked, clutching the rough wool blanket between my teeth and weeping uncontrollably.

CHAPTER 7

The next morning I could just walk to the bathroom. Even the weight of the sheet was painful. Georgios watched me lower myself slowly onto the bed with frightened eyes. At nine o'clock Dr. Simonata came to the house and put five little stitches in my finger. My mother hovered around nervously, but it didn't hurt that much; I was more interested in how he did it. He looked at my backside, prodding it gently and clicking his tongue, and gave my mother a prescription for some salve to rub on it. When I didn't turn up at school by noon, the truant officer came to our house to find out why.

The truant officer was Mr. Pevner, a thin man with a pointy nose who carried a black briefcase and wore a black wool coat all through the school year. We used to hide behind fences and shout, "Pevner pees in public!" when he passed, but really we were afraid of him. He had never been to our house before, and after he left my mother came upstairs looking worried. A few minutes later they called from school. The telephone was down in the dining room, but I could tell that it was Mr. Black. In furious broken English my mother blamed the principal for provoking my father into beating me. She told the story nonstop, lapsing into Greek when English failed her. "Blood, yes, plenty blood," she snapped, as if he was a moron not to be able to see it. "The finger? With his teeth."

I lay on my stomach, the only position I could bear. My father never even mentioned Tony—it was the public disgrace, getting caught by the principal, that he beat me for. My mother didn't blame my father for beating me—it was the principal's fault for sending the note home. But Mr. Black was no patsy either; everybody at school knew that. In a few minutes my mother was talking in a lower, more respectful tone, hesitating between words. Yes, she would tell my father right away. Yes, he would come today.

After she hung up I heard my father arguing with her and her angry replies. He stamped upstairs and went into his bedroom without looking at me. When he came out he was wearing his best suit, and he snarled at my mother to watch the store and not do anything stupid. When I heard the front door slam, I was exultant. I rolled over on my side without thinking and cried out involuntarily at the pain. In a few minutes my mother came up with a glass of milk and a plate of baklava. She sponged my welts again, but I realized that it would be a while before I could sit or walk normally. What would I say to people? I thought of Cissie Nolan and felt myself coloring; it was another disgrace. My mother changed my finger bandage and sponged my forehead and I fell into a fitful sleep.

I woke up to strange voices in the room. At first I thought I was dreaming, but when I opened my eyes Tony and Mark were sitting on chairs near my bed, eating *loukomades*. Georgios stood at the door watching. "Oh, shit," I said.

Tony grinned. "It's only us, greaseball." He still had a bandage on his head. "We came to see how you were," Mark said. "The club all says hello."

"Thanks." I was full of pee, hurting like hell, and embarrassed to have them see me. "It's okay," Tony said and pointed to his bandage. "It's like we were in the war." I had to smile; we did look like a junior version of one of those Red Cross posters of wounded soldiers. "What a jerk I was," I said.

Tony leaned forward and lowered his voice. "Listen, I got good news. Wait till I tell you the deal we made." He looked over his shoulder; Georgios had edged further into the bedroom. "Out," I said to him. He looked disappointed but he beat it instantly. "First of all," Tony began, "we can still work Hymie's route. Those two morons won't figure it out for a long time. We're averaging a hundred fifty a day. But that ain't the big news. We got a whole new route, a big one."

"I found it," Mark said proudly.

"Great. Where is it?"

"It starts at Twelfth and Pine. It's two hundred seventy papers."

"But how will we work a route up there and get back in time for school?"

"That's the best part," Tony answered. "We don't have to work it. We already bought the coupons on it for the whole contest."

"We bought them?"

"It's these two ham radio guys," Mark said. "They're both brains, they go to Central High. They worked out a way of delivering the papers real efficiently."

"And they're building a real efficient ham station." Tony winked at me.

"I get it. We're swapping a transmitter for the coupons."

"Right, except it's three transmitters. We're gonna make them two regular models, but you remember that guy at Eighth and Lombard who works under his car every Sunday?"

"The Czech guy?"

"Right. Well, he just bought a new Model T tourer, and it has the biggest magneto and coil set you ever saw."

"We already planned it," Mark said.

"This thing would blow you all the way to Front Street. It has a mahogany case and everything."

"How much is it worth?"

"Two hundred and seventy coupons a day for four months. We should have it Sunday night."

"You boys want some more *loukomades?*" My mother appeared at the door with a plate, and Tony jumped to his feet. "Sure, thank you, Mrs. Janus. They are real great." He gave her his best smile, and my mother melted just like Mrs. Goodman.

"What good boys. You have some too, Mark, I just made fresh." She pinched Tony's cheek. "What nice boys to come see Sol." It was a good thing there wasn't a whole family of Tonys, I thought; when he grew up the other politicians wouldn't have a chance. Tony's mother was thin and pale, and my sister had told me she lost two babies after Tony and then the doctors said she couldn't have any more. "You boys want to stay for dinner?" my mother asked.

"No thanks, Mrs. Janus, we have to go home soon." My mom smiled and went downstairs and we all leaned together again. "We can start collecting the Twelfth Street coupons as soon as we finish the transmitters," Tony said, "maybe by Wednesday." I knew I wouldn't be hustling any coupons by Wednesday. "I can wire the switches and binding posts in bed," I said. "What about the Mafia?"

"Not up there. It's a real classy neighborhood. The radio guys said the only people collecting coupons were kids and a few old ladies." Mark stood up and held out his hand. "Feel better, Sol." I had heard that Mark's father beat up on his mother, so he probably had a few welts himself.

My mom brought up some soup for dinner after the guys left. It was *mayeiritsa*, giblet soup, my favorite, and I was halfway through it when I remembered that it was still Lent and I wasn't supposed to be eating meat. Also I realized that my father must have come home after seeing Mr. Black while I was asleep. "What happened at school?" I asked. My mother put her finger to her lips. "Eat your soup. It's good? You want some more?" Nobody was talking. I settled for more soup.

CHAPTER 8

Saturday morning I could walk around a little. I locked myself in the bathroom, stood on the toilet seat, and looked at my behind in the medicine cabinet mirror. It was a mass of scabs and red welts, and there was one long deep crack that must have been made by the edge of the belt and that still bled when I poked it. It looked so bad I was frightened. What if it stayed that way? I had also noticed something else that worried me: I had no feeling at all in the tip of my index finger. The bandage was dirty where I had rubbed it, trying to feel some sensation. It was just like when your hand goes to sleep only it wouldn't wake up. When I went back to my room I found that I could sit on the edge of the bed for a minute if I lowered myself very gently. I rolled over on my stomach and thought about the contest.

I had put myself out of commission as a coupon collector, and I had almost put Tony out of commission, period. What a jerk. I should quit the club, I thought. I was sure the other guys would resent me if I didn't pull my weight. I wondered how many coupons we had. Tony kept them in a locked trunk in his basement with the bonus paper. The bonus paper! Suddenly I had an idea.

I called to my mom to send Georgios up when he came in from playing. It turned out he was helping my father unpack some tools in the store. I was surprised when he came right up. "Listen, Georgio, you want to help us?"

"Sure, what can I do?" He knew what I was talking about right away.

"Go over to Tony's and tell him to send back the bonus paper with you. Tell him I need it."

"Okay!" He was halfway out the door before I could call him back. "What?"

"Carry it carefully, understand? Don't open it, and don't show it to anybody, understand? Nobody. *Katalaveno?*"

"*Neh.*" He was downstairs and out the front door like a shot. As soon as the door closed I started to worry about all the things that could go wrong. What if he dropped it, or the Mafia guys caught him with it? I was still what-iffing when he came in out of breath and climbed on the bed. He took the paper out of his shirt. "Here it is. I ran all the way."

"Thanks, Georgio, that's good help."

"What're you gonna do with it?"

"I'm gonna try to figure out how they mark them."

"Can I see the page with all the coupons?"

"Sure." I turned to the beginning of the second section and opened the bonus page.

Georgios whistled. "Is it really a hundred?" He counted them off carefully. "Yep, a hundred. Think if they were dollars."

"Well they're not, they're just coupons. Okay, now let me work on it."

I put the paper back together, spread the front page on the floor next to the bed, and lay on my stomach with my head over the edge. I planned to study every line until I found the code marker. I figured that it had to be on the front or back page so they could spot it when they put them in with the regular papers. After half an hour I had a stiff neck and no results at all. I had expected to find a little star or asterisk at the edge of a line, but there weren't any. I went back to the top of the page and started to read the copy. I was about halfway down the page when I found two strange words at the end of a line: *etaoin shrdlu.* Hot dog, I thought, that had to be it! They even looked like secret code. The words were buried in the middle of the page where you had to know to look for them, and anyone reading the paper would think they were mistakes and skip right over them. The only thing was to check that they weren't on a regular paper. I hobbled to the top of the stairs and asked my mom for the latest *Clarion.* It took me about ten minutes to be sure that the front page had no *etaoin shrdlu* on it. Now, I thought, I could make up for not being able to collect coupons.

At three o'clock the whole club was assembled in my bedroom waiting to hear the big secret. Georgios was at the door listening, and this time I let him stay. "Okay," Tony said, "let's have it."

"It's two code words on the front page. I found them buried in an article at the end of a line. All you have to do is run down the right edge of the front page and if they're there it's a bonus paper."

"Wow," Harry said. "What are they?"

"*Etaoin shrdlu.*"

"What?"

"*Etaoin shrdlu.* See, they're right here."

Bobby squinted at the paper. "They do look like code words."

"Not bad, greaseball," Tony said.

"Uh," Mark said, "I think—" He stopped and looked uncomfortable.

"What is it?"

Mark turned red. "I think that's something else. I don't mean to—"

"Well what the hell else could it be?" Tony asked. "Look at it—they don't mean anything."

"No, they ain't words."

"Well if they ain't words, what are they?"

"They're filler slugs. My cousin Joe told me about it."

"What's a filler slug?" I asked.

"Well, when the typesetter runs out of words for a line and he can't fill it up he runs his fingers down the last two rows of keys on the type machine keyboard and it makes the letters *etaoin shrdlu*. The machine casts them in the slug with the rest of the line and they get printed in the paper."

"But I checked the front page of today's paper and it didn't have any."

"That just means they didn't run out of words on the front page. But I bet you there are some on other pages."

I was too worried to bet. "Okay, let's see," Tony said. Georgios was reading the front page, so we divided up the rest of the paper between us, and in about a minute Mark found one on page four and Tony found one on page nineteen: "The explosion of the volcano of Krakatoa in 1883 killed a total of thirty-six thousand, three hundred and eighty people. *etaoin shrdlu.*"

"Shoot," I said. "I thought I had it. It has to be something different."

"I found something different," Georgios said.

"Sure you did, kid."

"No, really, up here in the weather box. We had this word in school, *forecast.*"

"Well, so what?"

"Well, why do they spell it with a five instead of an *s*?"

"A five? Let's see." He handed me the page, and we all crowded around it. "You're right, it is a five. It almost looks like an *s*." I had gone right by it three times. Suddenly it was as clear as a bell: five, for *f*, for Fabulous Fifty! And it was in the weather box at the top right corner of the page where it would be easy to spot if you knew where to look. We checked the front page of the Saturday *Clarion;* forecast was spelled with an *s*. "We got it!" Georgios shouted, and we all cheered. "Too much noise," my father said from the doorway, and everybody froze.

CHAPTER 9

"Too much noise," my father repeated. They were the first words he had spoken to me since my whipping. For two entire days he had looked the other way every time he passed my door. "I'm sorry, Poppa, we'll talk quieter." He nodded and turned away. "How are you, Mr. Janus?" Tony piped up.

My father stopped and looked at Tony. "How? How I am."

"Hey Poppa, want to see a hundred coupons?" Georgios asked. I could have stuffed an eggplant in his mouth.

"What coupons?"

"You know, from the *Clarion* contest."

My father walked into the bedroom. Georgios held up the bonus page, and I held my breath. My father peered at the coupons. "It's worth money?"

"No, Poppa, but lots of prizes." Shut up, you little jerk, I thought.

My father shrugged. "Prizes you can't eat. You should save money." He looked at me for a second and then walked out. "Well," Mark said after a while, "now we know what to look for on the bonus papers. Maybe we'll get some on the new route."

"I found it," Georgios said.

"That's right, kid," Tony said. "Your brother will have to split some of his prizes with you when we win."

"Thanks a lot, politician," I said. "But everybody will help split."

"If we win," Bobby said.

Harry punched him on the arm. "Listen, we're gonna win," he said. "I ain't gettin' up early all these mornings for nothing."

Bobby looked uneasy. I winked at him. "You guys bring over the transmitters when they're ready to wire. I'll be able to get down to the bench tomorrow."

"Okay, Sol," Tony said. "I'll take the bonus paper back with me."

"That reminds me, I meant to ask you, how many coupons do we have?"

Tony looked up at the ceiling, thinking. "Let's see, with yesterday's—"

"We had a hundred forty-seven yesterday," Mark said.

"Right, so that makes three thousand, seven hundred sixty-one."

"Wow," Georgios said, "that's a lot."

"That's what you think," Tony said. "And that's a secret, kid. Don't you tell anybody how many we have, understand?"

"Okay, I won't." Tony looked at me questioningly.

"Don't worry, Georgio's okay. If he says he won't, he won't."

Tony glanced at my backside and nodded. "It's just that we still have a long way to go. It'll be better when we get the Twelfth Street route started. I'll bring the transmitters over Monday or Tuesday."

Everybody got up to leave. "Oh, I forgot," Bobby said from the doorway, "Cissie says hello."

I lay back in bed and thought about that while they

clattered down the stairs. *Hello,* she said. Cissie said hello to me. The thought of her voice actually saying it made my stomach tingle. I closed my eyes and thought of looking up Cissie's skirt from the janitor's window in the basement of school. In some funny way I could see Cissie's face, her beautiful turned-up nose and her freckles at the same time I could see up her skirt.

On Sunday Elena brought my lunch upstairs after she came home from church. She looked pretty, and she had put some flowers in a little vase for me. Mostly I thought flowers were sissy, but these made the boiled potatoes less boring. I was getting awfully tired of Lent food. Greek Orthodox Easter wasn't until May first, way after the Catholics and the Protestants, so there was a long time to go. Elena sat beside the bed while I ate. "Father Pappanikoulos asked for you."

"*Efkharisto.* He's a nice guy. Has he lost any weight?"

She smiled and shook her head. "After the service he bent down to kiss the little Andreades boy and he was as red as a tomato when he stood up."

"Did Poppa go to church?"

"No, he's been in a bad mood since—you know. Does it still hurt?"

"Only the big deep cut, it doesn't want to heal up. Well, there and my finger. I still can't feel anything in the tip."

"You poor baby." She leaned over and kissed my forehead like my mother did. It felt a little funny because she was only two years older than me.

"It's not so bad."

She shook her head disapprovingly, again like my mother. I guess two years made a big difference in how old you felt. Elena was taking a commercial course in high school, and Poppa had big arguments with my mother about how Elena should quit school and work in the store. My mother would yell back that Elena was smart and why shouldn't she finish high school like the boys, this wasn't the old country. Elena was the fastest typist in South Philly High, and she had two award certificates from the school district hung in her bedroom. Her boyfriend, Mark Theodouris, who worked in a carpenter shop on Passyunk Avenue, had framed them for her. "Was Mark in church?"

"We could only talk for a minute. You know how his mother is."

Mark was an only son like Tony, and his mother held on to him as if he were still a little boy. "She'll never change."

Elena laughed. "Don't worry, we won't give up so easily. I hear you have some problems like that."

"Me?"

"Cissie Nolan?"

I blushed in spite of myself. "It's nothing. How did you know about that?"

She laughed again. "Look at you. How could I not?"

"She doesn't know anything about me."

"That's what you think. Her sister told me she likes you a lot."

"Dammit, stop it!"

Elena sat back in surprise. "What's the matter, don't you like her?"

"It's nobody's business whether I like her or not. I haven't even talked to her and everybody knows more about it than me."

"I'm sorry."

"Aw, I'm sorry too. It's like when I hit Tony. I just want it to be private, you know what I mean?"

"Vevefsia, of course I do. You want it to be just you and her."

"Right. I wouldn't mind if it was like that, but this way it drives me nuts."

She reached over and held my hand. "Be patient. She does like you, but you'll have the same trouble as us."

"What trouble?"

"You think Poppa will put up with an Irish girl?"

"I don't care what Poppa thinks." The cut in my backside twitched when I said it. "He had his turn when he married Momma. What girl I like is my business, not Poppa's. That was the last time."

Elena knew what I meant. "I think you're right." She patted my knee and picked up the tray. "I'll see you later." She's really a nice sister, I thought.

"Your sister still going with that Theodouris guy?" Tony asked me in the workshop Monday night.

"Yep. Hand me the iron." Tony took the soldering iron off the gas ring and passed it to me. I had ordered it from the wholesale man; it had a slim copper tip half the size of the one my father used for repairing kettles. My father joked about big boys and little boys when it came, and he was still skeptical about the high-tin solder and the rosin I used for flux instead of acid. I rubbed the tip of the iron across the cake of sal ammoniac at the back of the bench and dipped it in the flux. It made a plume of acrid blue smoke, and when I touched the clean copper tip to the solder it tinned perfectly, a beautiful bright silver pyramid. Tony held the mounting board for the transmitter upside down while I soldered the binding post connections. "First class," he said.

"I bet that Czech guy's going to be pretty mad when he starts his car."

"He shouldn't know about it until Sunday."

"Sunday? What if he tries to drive it during the week?"

"Well, see, we swapped him. We took the big magneto out and put in an old regular-size one with separate vibrator coils. It oughta start okay, and he might not go under the hood until Sunday."

I was surprised. Tony had never done anything like that before; he just talked tough and swiped the magnetos. I put the iron back on the fire and stripped the insulation off the wires for the next connections. "Yeah, well, I figured it's a brand-new car and everything," Tony said.

"Uh-huh. Could you hand me the pliers?"

"And we never took anything on Sunday before. Look, I'm not gettin' soft, I've pulled twenty times more mags than you."

"I didn't say anything. If we had a spare, then it's okay with me."

"Well, Mark felt the same way. Besides, you should talk. You took that note home from school and gave it to your old man, and look at you. You shoulda dropped the note down the sewer. That's what I would've done."

"Can I have the iron again?" I soldered two more joints and gave it back to him. "Only four more to go. Boy, the case is really beautiful."

"Yeah, those suckers should love it. The other boxes look good too, I picked the best ones we had for them."

"Iron." I flowed two more joints. "You gonna deliver these tonight?"

"We set it up for tomorrow night. We can start Wednesday morning."

"It should be hot again now." Tony passed me the iron and I soldered the last two joints. "Okay, we can put it all together. And remember, no pliers on the hex nuts."

"Yeah, yeah, I remember. You're like a pain in the ass schoolteacher, you know that, Janus? I never would have put a perfectly good magneto and coil set back in that Czech's car if you weren't so stupid honest."

CHAPTER 10

The Twelfth Street hams had never seen transmitters like the ones we sent up; they loved them. "Suckers," Tony said. He and Mark started clipping the coupons from the new route on Wednesday, April 13, which was also the first day of the 1921 baseball season. The route was a coupon-clipper's dream. The *Clarion* driver left the papers in an alley off Lombard Street, and the two hams and Mark and Tony just sat there and cleaned out 270 coupons and then the other guys delivered the papers. They both had bikes with special baskets, and they could do the whole route in half an hour. "Those suckers are *fast*," Tony said when he brought my homework over Wednesday afternoon. "You'll see. By the way, how's your ass?"

"Better. I'm going to school tomorrow, but I can't do gym yet." I had to sit down carefully, but I was getting bored staying at home. My father still wasn't talking to me much.

"Well, it wouldn't have been worth cuttin' to see the ball game. Eleven innings the dumb Phillies hold them and then they lose it. And the A's! Jerks! We ain't gonna see any home teams in the series this year." He was probably right. The late edition of the *Clarion* confirmed that the Phillies had lost to the visiting New York Giants by a respectable 10 to 8, but the Athletics had been steamrollered by the

Yankees in New York, 11 to 1. "That Connie Mack doesn't know his ass from a hole in the ground," Tony went on. "Look at this." He picked up a thick bundle of coupons and tossed them over to me.

"How many?"

"Four twenty-three. Two-seventy from Twelfth Street and the rest from Hymie. It was Harry's day down here. That's what I call a good haul."

"You sure have been acting worried up to now."

"Well, there's stuff to worry about. When you gonna start collecting again?"

"How about Friday morning?"

"Great, we'll do Twelfth Street together. We're doubling up for a while because there's so many coupons. I hope Bobby and Harry will be able to handle those guys tomorrow."

At Thursday afternoon recess I asked Bobby how it went. "Okay. We got them all. You oughta see their bikes, they're brand-new Columbia Moto-Flyers. They have cross-brace handlebars and double-sprung saddles and rear carriers and a tank and horn and a headlight and a battery case and nickel-plated fenders and everything." That was the longest speech I had ever heard Bobby make. "How come you know so much about bikes?" I asked.

"Well, I never had one, but I like to read the catalogs."

"What're the guys' names, anyway?"

"Paul and Robert. Harry called the Robert one Bob and he said, 'Thank you, I prefer Robert if you don't mind.' They have pearl-handled knives too." The bell rang for class. "Oh, and Cissie says she's glad you're feeling better."

"Thanks," I said, trying to sound calm. I had been

looking for her all day without success. Just the mention of her name started the familiar tingling in my crotch. I put my hands in my pockets and thought about fire engines all the way to Mr. Feuter's room.

"*Carpe diem*," Mr. Feuter said after math. "Good advice."

"Is that what it means, good advice?"

"No, it means seize the day, in Latin." He wrote it on the board for me. "Make the most of every moment, take the chance when it comes along—that's what it means. If everyone took advantage of opportunities when they came along their lives would probably be different. Probably better." He looked up at the ceiling for a moment.

"Yes, sir. Thank you."

"Don't forget, you still owe me some homework."

"Yes, sir. I still can't write fast."

He looked at my bandage. "How are you, ah, feeling?"

"Fine, thank you," I said automatically. "Almost better."

Mr. Feuter shook his head and then smiled. "That's good, Sol. Remember, *carpe diem*."

Tony met me at six o'clock on Friday morning, and we trotted up South Street together. My backside hurt when I ran, but Tony kept a steady pace and I didn't want to slow us down. We went up Fourth and after we turned west on Pine the houses began to look nicer. We crossed Eighth Street two blocks south of St. George's Church, where Father Pappanikoulos had christened me. St. George's was the limit of my territory, the part of South Philly where every street and alley and vacant lot was mapped in my head. Farther up on Pine Street the houses had little gardens with freshly painted black-iron fences at the pavement edge and plane trees along the curbs in narrow beds of trimmed grass.

At Tenth Street the houses started to have polished brass number plates and window boxes filled with red geraniums. "That's one of their joints." Tony pointed at a paneled door painted a soft blue. It had a big brass knocker, and I slowed down enough to read the name *Fraser* in engraved script on the plate. "C'mon, we got work to do," Tony called.

In another minute we turned into the alley that ran from Pine to Lombard. I was amazed to see that the back fences were as freshly painted as the housefronts, in matching colors. There were no baskets of clinkers, no rusty garbage cans or piles of horse manure. What did they do with it all? Some of the houses were twice as wide as the others—you could tell by the paint and the curtains—and I realized that they must have broken through the connecting walls. Two houses for one family! "There they are," Tony said. "They been right on time every day."

As we puffed to a stop one of the boys looked at his wristwatch. I stole a glance at it. He was only in high school and he had his own wristwatch! "How're the transmitters working?" Tony asked the taller boy.

"Perfectly, thanks."

"This here's Sol Janus. He soldered them up."

"You do nice work." He held out his hand. "I'm Paul Fraser. Nice to meet you." Fraser was slim, a little taller than me, with smooth blond hair. "Hi, I'm Sol Janus." My tongue felt slow, like I'd had too much *retsina* or something.

"This is Robert Fish, my station partner."

"Hello." We shook hands and Fish smiled a little, but we didn't say anything. He was shorter than me, almost as thin as Tony, and his dark brown hair was as straight and as carefully combed as Fraser's. Both of them wore wool knickers, shirts and ties, and V-neck sweaters. Everything they had on looked brand-new.

"Let's go," Tony said. "We ain't got all day." He sat down on the pavement, took out his knife, and cut the twine around the first bundle of papers. I noticed Fish give a little sidelong smile to Fraser. We all began slitting coupons. I had honed a beautiful razor edge on my knife blades the night before, and I worked fast because it was uncomfortable squatting on the cold concrete. Fraser and Fish really did have pearl-handled knives, but I was cutting at least twice as fast as they were and checking the weather box on every paper besides. I noticed Fraser watching me from time to time. "That looks like a pretty good knife," he said.

"Regular Schrade, an eight-nine-two-four stock. Nothing special—a clip, a sheepfoot, and a pen."

"Is it new?" Fish asked.

"No, I got it when I was twelve." We cut in silence for a while, and as the clipped papers began to stack up Fish transferred them to the bike baskets. I tried not to pay attention to the bikes; they were all Bobby said and more. We were almost done when Fish asked me if I sharpened my knife myself. "Sure."

"Do you keep all the blades that sharp?"

I was down to the next-to-the-last paper. I glanced at the weather box and froze: FORECA5T. I looked at Tony, holding the paper by the weather box, and he caught on right away. "Uh, we need to take this whole paper."

"You can't," Fraser said. "We have just enough for our customers and we've never missed a delivery."

I looked at Tony questioningly and he shrugged; we had no choice. "Okay, but we have to take one page out of it. It doesn't have any news on it."

"It doesn't have any news? How do you know?"

"We just know."

I opened to the second section and there it was, a hundred coupons. "Son of a gun, look at that," Fish said. I turned the page to show that the back was blank and slit the whole thing out with one long sweep of my knife. Fraser and Fish were really surprised, you could see it on their faces. "Okay," Tony said, "I got the last one. Thanks, guys. We'll see you on Monday."

They stood up and finished loading the papers into their bike baskets. The bikes looked like they belonged in a fancy store window. If I felt like this, I thought, Bobby must feel like a bum. "Oh," I said, "you asked about the other blades." I opened the unused clip blade, pushed up my sleeve, and shaved a perfectly clean little square in the hair of my forearm. "See you next week."

Fish looked at my arm and then at my finger bandage. "Son of a gun," he said again.

CHAPTER 11

The next Monday morning I took my turn back on Hymie's route, and you could smell summer in the air. It made me think of polo shirts and Cissie. In fact just about everything made me think of Cissie. I gave the two mafiosi plenty of lead, and there was a new twist, a breakfast break. When they got to Swanson's Alley the hoods stopped at the end of it and waited. I doubled back a half block so I could look down the opposite end of the alley and saw Hymie come out of the Russian house with his giant buddy, both munching on *pirogs* and talking a mile a minute. Hymie's pants looked too short, and he didn't look so tiny next to the bear anymore. As they walked along, the top of his violin case swung back and forth in the *Clarion* bag with the papers. The hoods dropped into line again like a couple of windup toys, and I waited the usual two blocks behind and clipped the papers. I wondered how they could be so stupid. I guess they figured that if the papers made it to the doorstep they were safe, but I knew we couldn't go on forever. Even the dimwit Mafia bosses would figure it out eventually. The smell of the *pirogs* floated in the air behind Hymie, and by the time I finished collecting I was so hungry that I ate most of my lunch on the way to school.

When I got there I found a note waiting for me: *Please*

report to the principal's office. Uh oh, I thought, what now? On the way I tried to think of anything I could have gotten in trouble for. Mrs. Decker, the secretary, smiled at me and said to wait on the bench for a minute. Mr. Black came out and gave her some papers and called me into his office. I sat in the same chair, feeling wary. I hadn't been comfortable sitting down since the last time I had been there. "Well, Janus, you remember that I said I'd want to see you again."

"Yes, sir."

He looked at my finger. "Is that getting better?"

"Dr. Simonata said he would take the stitches out this week." But I still can't feel anything in it, I thought to myself.

"And the—other?"

"It's better than it was."

"Your father seems to take things very seriously."

"That's right, he does."

"I didn't expect his reaction when I sent that note home."

"It's not your fault. He just has a bad temper."

"Does he do that often?"

"When he gets mad." Never again, I thought.

"I see. How is Ammanati feeling? Are you still friends?"

"Sure, I told you, we're best friends. He's fine."

"Well, that's good. I just wanted to see how you were doing. Mr. Feuter says you're his best student."

"I already turned in the homework I owed him. I know the writing is rotten, but that's because of my finger."

"Yes, I understand. Well, if you ever want to talk about anything, please feel free to come and see me."

"Okay, thank you." Mr. Black stood up and I eased myself off the chair. He looked disappointed. I knew I was being crummy but I couldn't help it; if it hadn't been for him I wouldn't be beat up.

At lunchtime the club got together in the yard. "Those schmuck A's," Harry began. He and Tony began listing why they were schmucks, and Bobby grabbed me. "Did you see their brakes?"

"What brakes?" Oh yeah, bicycle brakes. Fraser and Fish. "No, I didn't."

"They're Paragon coasters, and you know what? They have two speeds! There's a lever on the handlebars that shifts them. Take a look next time."

"I will. Did you guys get all the coupons?"

"Sure. You know what? They asked if we all carried knives that were as sharp as yours, and if we had bigger ones for down here."

We all burst out laughing. "Look what I found up there," Bobby said. He took a small black ball out of his pocket. "It's a handball," Mark said.

"No it ain't, it's smaller, and besides, look at this." He dropped it on the ground and it hardly bounced at all.

"It's dead," Harry said. "It must be old. What good is that?"

"Well, it looks almost new. What do you think, Sol?" He tossed it to me. I caught it and squeezed it. "Beats me. It sure is hard." I tossed it back to him.

"Go out," he said. I turned around and trotted toward the center of the school yard. Bobby had the best pitching arm in the club. He cocked it and pointed farther out. I started to run, watching him over my shoulder. He threw, and I could see that it was going to be way over my head. I speeded up as fast as I could, jumped for the ball, and missed it. It bounced toward the wall of the school and disappeared into a crowd of girls. I skidded to a stop in front of them, out of breath. "Is this what you're looking for?" one of them said. She held out her hand with the ball in it, smiling. I gulped; it was Cissie.

"Yes." That's all? I said to myself. You're standing right in front of her and that's all you can say? "Uh, yes. We were playing catch with it."

"Would you like it back?" She smiled at me, two feet away; it was like the sun coming up in my stomach. She was so much more beautiful than I had imagined from a distance.

"Yes please, I would." She handed it to me very carefully, brushing her fingers across mine when she put the ball in my palm. She never took her eyes off my face or stopped smiling. I almost dropped the ball. "What a funny little ball," she said, and all the girls standing around her giggled.

"Actually, your cousin found it," I heard myself saying from far away. "Your cousin Bobby."

"You're Sol, aren't you?"

"Yes. And you're Cissie."

"Yes. I'm Cissie." The girls giggled again and right over our head the yard bell rang for the end of lunch. The girls started to walk away. I was rooted to the concrete. "See you later," Cissie called.

"See you later," I said mechanically. I looked down at the pavement where she had been standing. I felt the ball in my hand, running my fingers over it to see if I could feel where she had touched it. I could hear the very faint end of the bell vibration over my head. That was called resonance, Mr. Feuter said. Everything looked and sounded different. When I started to walk toward the school door it was like walking in slow motion, in some kind of special water where everything looked clearer than in air. She was so beautiful!

I sat down in Miss Geary's geography class. It was about Africa. I saw Cissie floating over the map of Africa, smiling at me. There were elephants and lions, giant waterfalls. "See you later," she said. The map at the front of the room was colored in pink and yellow and pale blue and green, funny colors that you only saw on maps and girls' dresses. "The Nile," Miss Geary said. It was a picture taken from an airplane, a narrow, dark line bordered with foliage and surrounded by pale, smooth hills of sand. "The pyramids," Miss Geary said. "And the Sphinx." I looked at the shadows of the pyramids and remembered the drawing I had seen of a lady sphinx in a library book. "You're Sol, aren't you?" "Sol . . . Sol . . . Sol Janus!"

I jumped. "Yes, ma'am." Everybody laughed.

"Can you tell us where the Sphinx is located?"

"Uh, in Egypt, ma'am." Everybody laughed again.

"Yes, we know that. But where in Egypt?"

"I don't know, ma'am."

"Do you know that this is a geography class?"

"Yes, ma'am."

"Perhaps you'd like an opportunity after school to learn just where the Sphinx is located."

"Yes, ma'am." The class roared. I was mystified; I wasn't trying to be a wise guy. Miss Geary filled out a detention slip. "This will help you learn the geography of the school office as well."

"Yes, ma'am." I came up and took it from her. Two or three people snickered. I wasn't even mad. Miss Geary looked at me with a puzzled expression.

Mrs. Decker was surprised to see me after school. I handed her the half-hour detention slip and sat down on the bench. It was wonderful to be able to sit and think about Cissie without anyone bothering me. After I had been there about ten minutes, Mr. Black came out to give Mrs. Decker some papers. He was very surprised to see me. "What's this for?" Mrs. Decker handed him the slip. "'Daydreaming in class. Did not answer when called on. Paid no attention to the lesson.' Is that accurate?"

"Yes, sir."

"Any excuse?"

"I was thinking about something else."

"Ah. Was it anyone I know?"

"Yes, sir."

"Today?"

"Yes, sir. At lunchtime. It was *carpe diem*. I just didn't realize."

"What was your geography lesson about?"

"Egypt. The Sphinx. I didn't know where it was. In Egypt, I mean."

"I see. Listen carefully. The Sphinx is at Giza, near the Great Pyramids, about five miles southwest of the center of Cairo. It was built around 2250 B.C., on the order of the pharaoh Chephren, and it's two hundred forty feet long and sixty-six feet high. Can you memorize that?"

"I'll try." He repeated it to me and on the third try I got it right. He folded up the detention slip and put it in his pocket. "Good. Now go home and make two copies of that, one for me and one for Miss Geary, and bring them in tomorrow morning. And try to think about her between classes instead of during them."

"Yes, sir, I'll try. I really will."

CHAPTER 12

Wednesday morning I went up to Twelfth Street by myself, and the first thing I did was check out the bikes. Bobby was right, they did have two speeds and coaster brakes. I was amazed that they could fit all those gears into that little hub. Fish looked edgy when I squatted down to look at his rear wheel. While we were cutting coupons I noticed Fraser watching me again. "That's a super knife."

"I just keep it sharp."

"Do you have a special kind of stone?"

"We have a Washita and a soft and hard Arkansas. We have a wet grindstone for big stuff, but you don't need that for a pocketknife. And we have leather strops for finishing."

"How come you need so many different kinds?" Fish asked.

"We have a hardware store; people are always coming in to have things sharpened. You need different stones for different edges."

"Could I try your knife?" Fraser asked.

"Sure." We traded for the next few papers. I knew the catalog listing of his knife by heart: Schrade 7426B Senator pattern, spear and small pen blades, brass linings, mother-of-pearl scales with nickel-silver bolsters. It was the top of the line, but the edges were pathetic. You practically had to saw the coupons out. "This is like using a razor," Fraser said.

"Can I try?" Fish asked.

"Sure." We swapped again and finished up the papers. Fish's knife was even duller than Fraser's.

"You sure it isn't some special steel?" Fish asked.

"No, it's just sharp. Speaking of sharp, how are you tuning your radios?"

"We use three variable condensers in series," Fraser said. I was jealous; that was out of the class of my toilet paper roller tuning coil, and about ten times as expensive. "Why don't you come over to my house on Saturday and I'll show you our rig?" Fraser said.

I was surprised, and I could tell by Fish's expression that he was too. I thought about it for a minute. "Sure, I could do that."

"And maybe you could teach us how to sharpen our knives like yours."

That sounded fair. "You got anything to sharpen with?"

"We have one of those gray stones with a wooden handle in the kitchen."

I laughed; that was the cheapest ten-cent sharpening stone made, worse than a toilet paper roller tuning coil. "I guess you'll have to come down to the store sometime." Fish glanced at Fraser, and I suddenly realized that they were afraid of us.

"Okay," Fraser said, "but you come up here one day first."

That day I tried to take gym for the first time since my beating. It didn't work out too well. My behind still felt stiff and sore, and when I tried to do squats the deep cut opened up and started bleeding again. It hurt a lot. Mr. Clark called me out of line and told me to go into his office. I was sure it was for a demerit. He came in after calisthenics and told me to turn around. I was embarrassed because the blood was showing through my gym shorts. "Damn this place," he muttered. "Until I tell you different, Janus, report to my office during gym class."

"Yes, sir."

"I hear you're pretty good with numbers." He tossed over a pile of file cards. "Divide these into six teams, and see if you can make up a schedule so every team plays every other team twice. It would be nice if it came out even."

"Yes, sir. But what about my gym grade? I'm supposed to graduate in June."

"Don't worry about it," he snapped, but I worried about it anyway.

That afternoon Dr. Simonata came over to take out my stitches. He was tall and gray-haired, and his dark suits and trimmed beard made him look like an ambassador. He spoke English with only a trace of a Greek accent. My mother said he was a saint; my father said he charged too much.

When he came into the house my mother practically curtsied. He washed his hands in the kitchen, and my mother fluttered around asking if he needed anything. He asked for a clean towel and told me to sit down next to him at the dining table and put my hand on the towel. "Have you had any trouble with the finger?"

"It started to bleed after I played stickball, so I put a new bandage on it."

"A good job, too." He unwrapped the bandage. "It looks fine, nice and clean." I looked at the crooked red scar and the ends of the stitches sticking up like unshaven hairs. I thought it looked awful. "You're a lucky fellow. A human bite can be terribly infectious." He opened a nickel-plated case full of tweezers and scalpels and things I didn't recognize. I guess if the tools hadn't been so interesting I would have been worried. "It will feel strange when I pull the stitches out, but it shouldn't hurt." He took out the pointiest pair of scissors I had ever seen and snipped the first stitch. Then he pinched one end of the suture—I liked that word right away—in a sort of tweezers with scissor handles. "Mosquito forceps," he said. He pulled the stitch out slowly and he was right, it did feel strange, like he was pulling out a piece of my finger, but it didn't really hurt. He slid the tiny scissors under the next stitch. "Iris scissors." They were beautiful, every surface was polished like a mirror.

"Are they expensive?"

He laughed. "All medical instruments are expensive. The people who make them think that doctors are million-aires. These are the best, from Switzerland." I watched him take out the next three stitches as carefully as the first. "Do you want to try one?"

"Sure, but I'm right-handed."

"That's no problem. You can do it with your left hand." He handed me the scissors, and when I put my thumb and index finger through the rings he smiled. "Not like that, you don't have any control." He showed me how to put my thumb and third finger through the bows and extend my index finger down along the point. "Now you can make it go where you want. Open a little—more—now slip the point under the stitch parallel with the scar. Good. Hold it steady and snip; that's it. Now take the forceps the same way." It was easy, even left-handed. I pulled the stitch through slowly and then pulled out the knotted end from the other side.

I heard a little noise behind me. My mother was watching with one hand over her mouth. She had the same expression as the first time she listened to my crystal radio. Dr. Simonata asked her in Greek for a clean cloth and soap and water. He sponged off the finger and dried it. "There, that's fine."

"There's one problem," I said. "I can't feel anything in the tip."

"I can believe it. You crushed a lot of nerves. The feeling should come back in a while."

"How long?"

"It depends how fast the neural paths are reestablished. Maybe a year." He got up and slapped me on the back. "You'd make a good doctor."

My mother was looking at him the way she looked at Father Pappanikoulos after a sermon that made her cry. *"To loghariasmo?"* she asked hesitantly.

"How can I give you a bill? He did all the work himself." He winked at me. "I need a screwdriver from Pavlos, though." Dr. Simonata packed up his instruments, shook hands with me, and went out to the store. I was sorry to see him go.

I gave Tony the 270 coupons that night, but I didn't say anything about going up to Fraser's house. "One of us can handle that route now," I told him. "Those guys aren't bad." Actually, I was beginning to like them. That was more than I could say for the A's, who lost to the Yankees again on Thursday, 6 to 1, and stuck themselves right in the American League cellar.

CHAPTER 13

Saturday was another beautiful spring day. I trotted up to Twelfth and Lombard breathing in the delicious smell of frying scrapple and budding trees. A family on Eighth Street was having bacon for breakfast. Only one more week to our Easter; I could practically taste the roast lamb. When I got to the drop-off, the papers were already there. I started clipping and a few minutes later Fraser and Fish rode down the alley from Pine Street. "Sorry we're late," Fraser said, "we stayed up last night trying for DX's."

"Any luck?"

"We got two guys from West Hartford. Those guys must all have big rigs because the ARRL is there."

"We almost had one from Concordia, Kansas," Fish said, "but we couldn't hold his signal. He was really fast."

"I tried to sharpen my knife last night," Fraser said. He handed it to me. The spear blade was sticky and had sort of a scratchy edge on it. "What'd you use?"

"That kitchen stone. I remembered reading that you should use oil, so I used salad oil."

"Oh boy. You should have waited for me. We can fix it down at the store, though. Let's get through the papers." There were a few less *Clarion*s on Saturday—257 coupons —and in twenty minutes we had the whole thing finished. I waited while they delivered and then came back.

"I'll see you guys later," Fish said. "I'm going clothes shopping with my mom." He waved and pedaled away easily.

"I have to put my bike in the garage," Fraser said. He walked it so we could talk. I desperately wanted to ride it, but I was afraid to ask. We turned into the alley behind Pine Street and stopped at the fourth house down. Two wide doors in the back fence were standing open, and a big maroon Chandler sedan was idling outside the garage. It was even shinier than Fraser's bike. A tall bald man in a tan suit was fiddling with the spark advance lever. "Hello, Dad," Fraser said.

"Well, hello, Paul. Papers all finished?"

"Yes, sir. This is my friend Sol."

Mr. Fraser looked me over and held out his hand. "How do you do, Sol?"

"Fine thank you, sir." I guessed that was what I was supposed to say. Nobody had ever asked me how I did except on tests.

"Are you at Central?"

"No, sir, at the Foote School."

Mr. Fraser picked up a pipe from the Chandler's ashtray and scratched his ear with it. "Well, I can't say I know it. I'm going down to the office, Paul. I should be home by three. Take care of things."

"Okay, Dad."

"Nice to meet you, Sol." Mr. Fraser lit his pipe, put the car in reverse, and backed into the alley. The engine sounded very smooth as he drove away.

"C'mon." Fraser wheeled his bike into the garage and stopped it by the side wall. "Hold it a second." I steadied it while he unhitched a rope from a cleat and lowered a varnished pole from the ceiling. He swung two hooks under the tank bar—they had leather sleeves so they wouldn't scratch the paint—hoisted the bike up about a foot, and fastened the rope again. I was mystified. "It keeps the tires from getting flat spots," he said.

"Oh, right." I tried to make it sound obvious. "What does your father do?"

"He's a lawyer. He does corporate law mostly." He opened the back door and we walked through a screened porch and into the kitchen where a black lady in an apron was rolling out dough on a board. At least that looked familiar. The kitchen smelled delicious. "Well, Mr. Paul, I bet you're hungry for a change," she said.

"I'm always hungry, Velma. This is my friend Sol, and he's hungry too, aren't you?"

"Well . . ."

"Course you are," Velma said. "Every growing boy is hungry. Got some, let's see, got some almond cookies, got some bacon strips, got some cinnamon toast. We're havin' chicken à la king for lunch. What you in the mood for?"

It was like a restaurant. Fraser looked at me. "I'd like some cookies and milk, if there's enough, I mean. Please."

"Enough!" Velma started to laugh; she had a deep laugh like a man's. She pointed to a big can like the one Mrs. Goodman kept potato chips in. "All cookies, top to bottom. Made a new batch yesterday." We sat down at the kitchen table, and Velma poured us each a glass of milk and put a big plate of cookies between us. They were different from anything my mother made, thin and crisp with a taste of vanilla and a shiny almond in the middle. "You like 'em, huh?" Velma asked when I was eating my fourth.

"They're delicious."

"All Mr. Paul's friends like 'em. Mr. Sol, that right?"

"Yes, ma'am."

She laughed that wonderful laugh again. "Listen to him! Velma is just fine, honey."

"Thanks, Velma," Paul said. "C'mon, let's go up to my room." I followed him through a breakfast room and a dining room with a big crystal chandelier into the front hall. "Paul?"

"Yes, Mom," he called up the stairs.

"Wait there, dear, I'll be right down." Mrs. Fraser's voice was so polished it made me nervous. But that was nothing compared with how nervous I felt when she came down the stairs. The mothers I knew on South Street looked like mothers: Most of them were plain, heavy women with wiry black or gray hair that they kept in a bun. They wore housedresses, aprons, dark stockings, black shoes, thick wool coats, kerchiefs, and shawls. I had never seen one wear makeup. Mrs. Fraser was so beautiful that I couldn't believe she was anyone's mother. She wasn't beautiful like Cissie— that was different because Cissie couldn't help being beautiful. When Mrs. Fraser came down the stairs it was like Mary Pickford was walking into the room. I thought my sister Elena was pretty, and I knew she wore makeup at school secretly, but if she had to stand next to Mrs. Fraser in front of a mirror she would probably have started to cry.

"This is my friend Sol," Paul said.

Mrs. Fraser and I looked each other over. I was wearing a clean school shirt, nearly new corduroy knickers, cotton socks, and brown street shoes. I had to persuade my mother to let me wear such good clothes to run around the streets on Saturday. Mrs. Fraser was wearing a slim pale-yellow dress like the ones in the ads in the *Clarion* and matching little high heels. She had bobbed blond hair, blue eyes, a nose almost as cute as Cissie's, and the most elegant silk-stockinged legs I had ever seen. I thought she looked like Paul's older sister. She smiled and held out her hand. "How do you do, Sol?"

"Fine, thank you, ma'am." I prayed that that was right.

"What's your last name, Sol?"

"Janus. Sol Janus." My tongue felt clumsy.

"Janus. Is that a Jewish name?"

"No, ma'am, it's Greek. My real name is Solon. Solon Demetrios Janus."

"How unusual! I read some Homer in college, but that was a translation. Can you read Greek?"

"Yes, ma'am, but Homer is classical Greek. We speak modern Greek."

"Sol made our transmitters," Paul said. "He does beautiful work."

"You boys do seem to enjoy this radio business. I must say it's all—"

I closed my eyes without meaning to because I was so tired of hearing what I knew she was going to say. Mrs. Fraser stopped in mid-sentence. ". . . very mysterious," she finished. When I opened my eyes, she was smiling straight into them just like Cissie had. I smiled back, feeling foolish. "Barbara Caldwell is picking me up to go shopping," she said to Paul. "You have a nice afternoon." She leaned over and he gave her a kiss on the cheek. "I should be back by four. Nice to meet you, Sol."

"Nice to meet you too, ma'am."

We started up the stairs, my feet sinking into the thick maroon carpet. I was so keyed up that it could have been a path into the jungle. The banister was polished mahogany, and everything I touched or looked at was shinier, softer, brighter colored, different from the things I knew. We climbed two flights of stairs. "They let me move my room up here last year," Paul explained. "I wanted to be close to the roof."

"Wow," I said. I couldn't help it. Paul's bedroom was bigger than our dining room at home, which was where my whole family lived, ate, read, did homework—everything. This room was papered with a bright blue-and-white pattern. It had two beds, a wall of white-painted book-shelves, a desk, a fireplace, an easy chair, and a worktable, covered with radio equipment, against one wall. Some of the shelves had toys on them that I had only seen in expensive catalogs.

"Where'd you get the train?"

"My uncle brought it back from Europe. It's German, from before the war. Take it down if you like."

I lifted the engine down carefully. It was a dark green steam-powered model of a German locomotive, and it made American toy trains look like tin cans. "I didn't know they made trains like this, I mean except for in a museum."

Paul laughed. "We'll set up the track and run it one day. Come over and look at our rig."

I put the engine back—there was a battleship that looked just as beautiful on the next shelf—and went over to the station. It was funny, they had expensive equipment, but there were a lot of rough spots. I could tell they didn't know how to solder, because many wires were twisted together or connected with fahnstock clips. The antenna came in under the window frame, and I could see the down-lead outside swinging loose against the house. "You have some neat stuff," I said. "The key is beautiful."

"You have to try it. We don't get the kind of signal that we should, though."

"That's because there are a lot of leaks. How come you don't insulate the antenna down-lead and solder the connections? Your dad could teach you how."

"My dad!" Paul laughed. "He can barely put in a light bulb. Besides, he's not home much. He has to travel a lot for business, and he and my mom go out most nights."

"Well, I could teach you. It's easy. We can straighten out some of this stuff right now." For the next two hours we cleaned up the leads and rewired the station. We were just ready to go out on the roof to check the antenna when Velma called up the stairs. "Lunch, Mr. Paul and Mr. Sol."

"Okay, Velma, we'll be right down," Paul called. He opened what I thought was a closet door and there was a bathroom, connected right to his own bedroom. "Want to take a leak before lunch?"

"Sure." We went in and he washed his hands while I peed. He waited while I washed mine. "Go on down, I'll be right with you." I went down the stairs, looking into rooms as I passed them. It was worse than going up because I could take my time; no matter where I looked, everything was perfect. A *Clarion* was lying on the hall table and I unfolded it to check the baseball scores. Suddenly I noticed that the front page was uncut, complete with a Fabulous Fifty coupon. So they held out papers for their parents!

That's right, the parents probably wouldn't like the deal that they had made with us.

"Here I am," Paul said. "C'mon, I'm famished." I followed him into the breakfast room, where two places were set. A glass of milk and a plate of salad were beside each place, and there was a basket of hot biscuits and a steaming tureen. It smelled wonderful. Suddenly I felt revolted. "Look, I'm sorry, but I can't stay."

Paul looked shocked. "Why not? Do you feel okay?"

"Well, it's still Lent, and I can't eat any meat."

"That's okay, Velma will make you something else."

I stood up. "No, I better go. Thanks for everything."

"Don't go, we can make something else, really."

"I have to."

"Well, promise you'll come back. I'll come down and visit you if you like. Let's set a date now."

Anything to get out of here, I thought. He brought in a calendar from the library, and we picked Saturday, June 11, as far away as I could make it. Paul let me out the front door. "Tell Velma I'm sorry," I said. As soon as he shut the door I started running, and I ran all the way home. I was completely out of breath when I came in, and I ran straight through the house and up to my bedroom and slammed the door. Elena was standing in the kitchen doorway when I went by. In a minute I heard a knock on my door. "Who is it?"

"It's me. Can I come in?"

"If you want." I was lying on the bed face down and I didn't look up when she sat down next to me. "What is it, Sol, is it Cissie?"

"No, dammit!" I punched the pillow with all my might.

"I'll never be anything, I'll never be any good, I'm just a schmuck like those stupid A's!"

"Oh, Sol." She rubbed the back of my neck and I couldn't help it, I started to cry like a dumb little kid.

CHAPTER 14

I felt a little better after I told Elena about Paul's house. "They were really nice to me, but after a while I couldn't stand it."

"I know," she sighed, "it's just different." I had to settle for that.

The next day was Palm Sunday, and after church I worked on the volleyball schedule for Mr. Clark. It took me three tries to get a round-robin that would work without any byes. Tony came over that night and we sat outside and talked. "If I was president, I'd have daylight saving time all year," he said.

"I'll remind you. You really want to be president?"

"I guess I'd be a great baseball player like Babe Ruth if I could be anybody."

"I'd rather be a great scientist."

"You mean like that kook Einstein? The paper says there's only ten guys in the world that understand him. You wanta be like that?"

"I'm not smart enough. I could never be like him."

"Yeah, but who'd wanta? They don't make any dough anyway."

"Speaking of dough, how many coupons do we have?"

"Counting today, eight thousand, eight hundred seventy-nine."

"That's pretty good."

"I'm glad for daylight saving, though. It'll be darker in the mornings for a little. People get itchy when it gets light early. It's gonna be hard working Hymie's route in the summer when the kids are sleepin' out on the roofs."

He was right; I hadn't thought of that. "Maybe we can find another route like Twelfth Street."

"How many hams with paper routes do you think there are? I figure it must have been a miracle. Me and Bobby have been saying extra Hail Marys in church ever since we got it."

That was another new number. The contest seemed outside of religion to me. "There aren't as many bonus papers around either."

"Yeah, the whole thing's slowed down. Everything's stayin' the same."

"Stable."

"Yeah, whatever. Nobody's givin' anything away, that's for sure."

Even with a double order of potato chips we couldn't think of any new ideas at the meeting Tuesday night, but it was a good day for me anyway. First, I gave Mr. Clark my volleyball schedule. Elena typed it at school for me, and I ruled a border around it with red ink. "No byes, eh?" Mr. Clark said. He tacked it up on the bulletin board and stood back and looked at it. "That's pretty good, Janus."

"I ought to be able to do squats soon," I said.

"Don't rush it. I had a cut like that once. I hit a board at the edge of the long-jump pit in the Penn Relays. It took a long time to close up. No byes, how do you like that?" he said again. I guessed my gym grade was going to be okay.

The other good thing that happened was at lunchtime. I still couldn't play buck-buck, so we played catch with the ball Bobby had found. I missed a couple of catches because of looking for Cissie, and when the bell rang at the end of lunch I managed to get right next to her. She was at the back of her crowd of girlfriends, and we squeezed our hands together for a second. Just when we separated to go down different halls she twirled around like a little girl, and in the second she was facing me she blew me a kiss. I needed a whole hook and ladder brigade to get into respectable condition for Mr. Feuter's class.

By Friday of that week I was certain that we would never get the World Series in Philadelphia. The A's were holding on to the cellar as if they were getting paid for it. On Wednesday the Phils lost to Boston 10 to 6, on Thursday they lost again 6 to 2, and by Good Friday they had slid down to seventh place where they could feel comfy with the A's. "Jerks," Tony said, when I walked over to his house after dinner. I was thinking about one more day before giblet soup and roast lamb. "C'mon down to the basement, I wanta show you something." I followed him to the corner where we kept the coupons in his parents' big roundtopped trunk. He took the carpet off the lid, unlocked it, and opened it. I was surprised to see that the coupons were starting to fill it up. They were stacked in neat rows, each bundle of a hundred tied with string. Tony handed me a sheet of paper with the running total. "Take a look."

"Ten thousand, five hundred and fifty-nine. We broke ten grand!"

"That's right. Remember at the beginning when you said we couldn't do it? I still ain't sure we're gonna make it, but ten grand is a big number. You wouldn't feel bad to say you got ten grand of anything." I thought about that before I fell asleep. Tony was right, I couldn't remember any number in my life as big as ten thousand. I hadn't even thought about Cissie that many times.

In a Greek Orthodox house Holy Saturday was devoted to two things: cooking and baking. You never saw so much bread being kneaded, eggs being dyed red, lamb being cut up and tied and skewered. There were certain older lady relatives who only appeared at Easter to work in the kitchen. They would pinch your cheeks and then they would roll up their sleeves and make some special kind of bread or dessert. I don't know what they did the rest of the year. You could get a rash from all those old ladies pinching your cheeks.

Saturday night was the first of May. It was a warm night, but we had to wear our best suits to Easter service, and they were heavy blue wool. Georgios and I sat around itching in our knickers. I tied my tie and his, and my mother kept trying to brush his hair. Elena wore a new dress, and I noticed that my father wore the belt with the silver wire rings. My bottom twitched when I saw it. He was still not talking to me much, and on the way to church he walked ahead of the family, not talking to anyone.

Our service began at eleven o'clock. At Washington Square we became part of a stream of people heading toward St. George's. As we went into church the acolytes standing by the doors handed each of us a long white candle. I was happy to see that Mark Theodouris was in the row in front of us, not far from Elena. He turned around and smiled at our family. My father just stared straight ahead at the altar.

The service started, and that year it seemed different than I remembered it. I guess it was me that was different. Father Pappanikoulos had a deep, powerful voice, and there was something about the service—the warmth, the dark, all of us so close together—that made his voice feel as though it was partly inside you. As it got closer to midnight my mother started to cry, and I reached across Georgios and held her hand. Elena put her arm around her from the other side. One by one the candles around the church were put out, until just before midnight there was only a single one left burning in front of the altar. Then, while Father Pappanikoulos chanted, an acolyte lifted his brass snuffer and lowered it slowly over the flame, and the whole church went black. There was only Father Pappanikoulos's voice in the dark, and then that stopped. Everyone held their breath. Christ was in the tomb.

Suddenly there was a tiny flicker of flame in the altar enclosure. Father Pappanikoulos stood holding a lighted candle which seemed to have appeared in his hand by magic. *"Thefte, lavete phos ek tu anaspiru photos,"* he sang: Come, receive ye the light from the rekindled light. He came down from the altar, and one by one the people at the end of each row lit their candles from Father Pappanikoulos's as he walked slowly down the aisle toward the rear of the church, followed by the acolytes and the congregation. I lit my candle and passed the flame to Georgios, and we followed the procession. Mark and Elena slipped past us in the aisle, and I saw Mark take her hand and lead her ahead in the crowd.

By the time we reached the front door, the church was shimmering with candlelight. Father Pappanikoulos waited at the top of the steps beside the door until the whole congregation was outside the church in a great silent half circle, everyone as close to his neighbor as he could get, all of us holding our candles up. I knew that many boys in the crowd were also holding firecrackers and cherry bombs in their other hands, waiting. Father Pappanikoulos stepped to the center of the steps, framed by candles on all sides. He held out his hands to us and to heaven. *"Christos anesti!* Christ is risen!"* he proclaimed. The steeple bell pealed and suddenly the air was full of explosions. A brilliant red rocket zipped into the sky overhead and burst in a gorgeous shower of pink and purple streamers. Firecrackers went off everywhere, around the crowd, under people's feet. The boys shouted, women and girls screamed, people hugged one another, the church bell kept clanging over the firecrackers, the din was terrific. It was the real new year, and somehow, for me, it was the beginning of a new life.

CHAPTER 15

Father Pappanikoulos was a baseball fan, but I bet he felt that God wasn't paying much attention to baseball that summer. At the beginning of June the Philadelphia teams were one game away from total disgrace. The A's were still in last place, and the Phils were in seventh, hanging a rung above the National League cellar by their fingernails. Tony had demoted the A's from schmucks; he couldn't mention them without a string of swearwords. The Cleveland Indians and the Pittsburgh Pirates were in first place in their leagues, the Yanks and the Giants were in second, and they were all playing hardball.

On June 2 the Phillies lost both games of a doubleheader to the Giants, 9 to 2 and 8 to 3, and slid down to eighth place. Now we had a clean sweep of the booby slots. I bet the guys at the *Clarion* that thought up the Fabulous Fifty contest were tearing their hair out. As soon as they had nothing to lose, both Philadelphia teams drove the fans nuts on June 4 by winning two tough games. The Phils beat the Cardinals 6 to 5, and the A's!—the dumb A's hit seven homers, which tied the major league record, and sank Detroit 15 to 9. They stayed in the cellar anyway; it would have been better if they had lost.

School seemed to be running down as the weather got warmer. The most important thing that happened was that

Mr. Black called me into his office and told me that he and Mr. Feuter had written recommendations for me and that I was accepted to Central High, the college-preparatory high school. I did want to go there instead of to South Philly High like the other kids, but the teachers had more to say about it than I did. Outside of school we kept collecting coupons and spent all our spare time playing stickball.

The end of that year felt different because we were graduating from the Foote School. Graduation was on June 21, and early in the month we began rehearsals for it. The kids in the band were excused from classes so they could practice. From outside the auditorium you could hear them working on the same piece over and over. Mr. Feuter said it was called "Pomp and Circumstance." It sounded like they would never get it right.

My behind was all better, although I had a scar from the deep cut. I still couldn't feel anything in my fingertip, and I had almost forgotten about it. It was funny—after I figured out the volleyball schedule for Mr. Clark, he never asked me to take gym with the other kids again, even when I told him I was healed up. He made me sort of an assistant, and I wrote all the game schedules for the rest of the term. I even helped transfer the marks from the day sheets to the grade book. I had gotten an *A* on my last report card, but there were no grades next to my name since my beating.

Before I knew it, it was June 11, the day I had promised to sharpen Paul's and Robert's pocketknives and teach them to solder. No one in the club knew they were coming to the store. I especially didn't want Tony hanging around making wisecracks. When I told my mom and dad that my friends from Twelfth and Pine were visiting and I wanted to use the workbench, my dad grunted and my mom invited them to lunch. I told Georgios to stay out of my hair all day. I wasn't sure about any of it.

We had agreed on ten o'clock. At five of ten I was waiting in front of the store. It was a hot, sticky day, and the street was crowded with pushcarts. At ten sharp Paul and Robert rode up on their bikes. I could follow their path through the crowded street by the trail of light-fingered kids giving the bikes the once-over. You didn't see bikes like that on South Street. "Here we are," Paul said. He looked around as one of the urchins ran a grimy hand over the gleaming rear fender of his bike. "Hi," I said. "You better bring those inside."

They wheeled the bikes into the store, following me. My father was selling some guy a monkey wrench. On an ordinary day my friends and I walked by my father fifty times; he was used to ignoring us when he was making a sale. This time he stopped in the middle of a sentence and stared at Paul's and Robert's Columbia Flyers with an open mouth. He knew what those bikes cost; nothing like them had ever crossed our doorstep before. "Put them over here," I said, and Fraser and Fish followed me, parking the bikes where they would be out of the way. In the dark interior of the store the nickel headlights and shining red-and-blue frames glowed like jewels in a cave. I saw Georgios looking at them from the back counter like he couldn't believe his eyes. My father was still standing there speechless. "These are my friends Paul Fraser and Robert Fish," I said.

He shook hands with them silently, looking up at them as

if they were some kind of mysterious beings. "It's nice to meet you, Mr. Janus," Robert said.

"Nice to meet you," my father muttered, looking sideways. I had never seen him lose his self-confidence before.

"We're going to sharpen our knives and do some soldering," I said.

"Good, good," he said. He turned back to his customer and started talking about the wrench again. In a moment he stopped and called after us, "Be sure to get to eat. Tell your mother."

"I will." I guessed she had probably made enough food for the staff of the *Clarion*. We went into the workroom and I took the covers off the Washita and Arkansas stones and spread a film of Nyoil over them. Paul and Robert took out their knives and laid them on the bench. The hinge on Paul's spear blade felt as if it were lined with sandpaper. I opened the pen blade and made them look inside. "Opening two blades at the same time isn't smart, but see all the junk in there? You have to clean out all that grit and lint because it ruins your hinges." I swabbed the inside of the case and flushed the hinges with oil until the blades folded smoothly. "The salad oil didn't want to wipe off," Paul said.

"No problem, I can dissolve it with acetone." I cleaned the sticky coating off. The blades were as dull as dinner knives. "Okay, the first thing is to work up a clean bevel on both sides." I stroked the spear back and forth on the Washita, alternating sides and keeping the angle nice and shallow. "That looks hard," Paul said.

"It takes some practice, but you'll be able to do it. You just concentrate on keeping the blade at the same angle to the stone and letting your wrist bend. See the black stuff in the oil? That's ground-off steel. Okay, now you hold the edge in line with a light and look for reflections from the edge. If you see any, you work on the bevel until they disappear."

"Can I try?"

"Sure. Feel this first, though. Not like that, crossways. You'll cut yourself on any good edge if you run your finger along it."

"It feels sharp but sort of raggedy." Paul handed the knife to Robert.

"That's how it's supposed to feel after the Washita. It's called a wire edge. Usually it's rougher on one side."

They took turns putting new bevels on the spear blades, and then I showed them how to hold the pen blade at a shallower angle. "This feels sharper than when I got it," Paul said.

"That's nothing. Now we take off the wire edge." I started working the spear blade on the hard Arkansas stone. I loved using it. Ours was a silky pearl-white and shaped sort of like Pennsylvania. My father had carved a matching recess in a block of mahogany for it. I showed them how to stroke lighter and lighter, just kissing off the wire edge. "Wow, feel it now," Paul said.

"We're not done yet." I pulled up the leather strop and polished off the edges. We kept some tissue paper in a bench drawer, and I took a piece out and held the edge of Paul's pen blade against it. "Watch." The blade cut a clean slit as I pulled the paper toward me. "That's a pretty good edge."

"Pretty good! That's like a razor!"

"That's how I like to keep them." I took out my own

knife and cut all the way across the sheet of tissue. I have to admit that I had worked on it for half an hour before they came, and Dr. Simonata could have used it for surgery. My mom opened the door to the workroom. "You boys would eat some lunch?"

"Sure, Mom, I'll clean this up. We can do the soldering later." This was the part I had been dreading. I cleaned off the stones and workbench, took a deep breath, and led the way into the dining room. I saw every spot on the carpet, the faded wallpaper, the cracked veneer on the table where my father had hit it. When we went upstairs to use the bathroom, I saw Paul glance at the icons on the wall of my parents' bedroom.

Usually my friends ate in the kitchen, but today my mom had set three places at the dining table. There was a Greek vase I didn't remember seeing before filled with flowers in the middle of the table, and a runner under it embroidered with a design of porpoises. The usual delicious smells were coming from the kitchen, but I was so nervous I could hardly taste anything. I have to say that Fraser and Fish were better sports on South Street than I was on Pine Street. They ate *avgolemono* and baked lamb and moussaka as if they loved it, they had seconds, and they had my mother practically crying with delight from their compliments. "Nice boys," my mother said, "such nice boys. Next time I make you *mayeiritsa,* Sol's favorite. You'll like."

Robert took a third piece of baklava. "I thought I had tried everything sweet," he said. "But this beats it all."

"That's one thing about Fish," Paul said. "If he won't eat it, you can always dip it in sugar."

After lunch we went back to the workroom and I taught them how to solder. I felt a twinge of jealousy when Paul said his father had bought him an American Beauty electric soldering iron. My father still thought that soldering radio connections and copper pipes was the same thing. He was almost cheerful when he said good-bye to Paul and Robert late in the afternoon. My mother brought out two little packages of baklava for them to take home. When they rode away she stood in the doorway watching. "Such nice boys," she said.

"They're okay," I said. "I have plenty of nice friends." She looked at me with a puzzled expression. I went upstairs, shut my door, and lay down on the bed. I felt like I had been playing world-championship stickball for eight hours.

CHAPTER 16

I had once read a book in the library about how lobsters shed their old tight shells and grow fast before the new ones harden. The week before graduation the Foote School felt like an old shell to me. Some of the teachers let us draw pictures and talk right through class. One day I was delivering a note and Miss Gregory, my first-grade teacher, saw me passing and motioned to me to come in. "Hello, Sol, I understand you're graduating."

"Yes, ma'am, I am." She was a tiny, plump woman with a warm smile; I could remember looking up at her from those midget desks and thinking how tall and pretty she was. "This is Sol Janus," she said to the class. "He's graduating, and I hope you all do as well here as he has. Let's say good luck to him." She held up a finger to lead them, and the kids shrilled "Good—Luck!" and started giggling. One little girl with pigtails grinned at me and said "Good luck, you big monster," and the class shrieked with laughter.

Tuesday morning I woke up early enough to do Hymie's route, but we had agreed that we wouldn't try to clip it that day. Paul and Robert were going to save the Twelfth Street coupons for us. I lay awake thinking about all the things that had happened in the past few months: the *Clarion* contest, hitting Tony, my beating, Cissie, meeting Paul and

Robert. It felt as if my life had speeded up out of control. I heard the milkman coming down the street and thought that Hymie's customers were going to faint when they got their papers with coupons in them this morning.

We didn't have to be at school until nine-thirty. I took a long time getting dressed and ate a slow breakfast, but the time crawled. My suit seemed to have shrunk since Easter; the jacket wouldn't button and the knickers pulled at my knees. I met Tony and Harry on the way to school, and Mark and Bobby were waiting for us in the yard. We gawked at each other in the unfamiliar clothes. Some of the eighth-grade girls seemed to have grown up completely in one weekend. Quite a few of them had managed to sneak on some makeup. I looked for Cissie, but I didn't see her before the bell rang and we filed into school.

We waited in Miss Geary's room. The marching instructions were written on the board in three colors of chalk, and when we got to the bottom it said, "Congratulations and Good Luck to My Best Geography Class!" I remembered messing up the Sphinx and Giza. After the instructions Miss Geary made a little speech. She was wearing a light purple dress with a flower pinned on it. When I looked down I realized that she was wearing high heels and that she had pretty legs. Miss Geary! In three years I had never noticed that she had legs at all. When we lined up in the hall by size, I was the last one. Miss Geary walked beside me, and she smelled almost like Mrs. Fraser.

At five after eleven the orchestra started "Pomp and Circumstance." Except for one trumpet cracking, they did it pretty well. I caught my breath as we walked into the auditorium. It was full of people from wall to wall, everyone dressed in good clothes, just like at church. Miss Geary had told us to watch for our row and not look around, but it was impossible; we all tried to find our families. I didn't see my parents, but I caught a glimpse of Cissie going down the opposite aisle. She was wearing a yellow dress and she looked like an angel. We passed a row with two men towering above everyone else, and I recognized Hymie's Russian friends. It was a wonder they could fit in the seats.

We found our rows, filed in, picked up our programs from the seats, and remained standing, as instructed. The orchestra finished, we sat down, and I looked through the program. Everyone was talking so much that I didn't expect to hear any of it, but the noise stopped when Mr. Black walked up to the podium. He looked very distinguished. He introduced Mr. Shelley, who led the orchestra, and then he introduced a minister from Old St. Mary's, who gave a prayer of dedication. Mr. Black made a short speech about the rewards of higher education, and how he hoped we would distinguish ourselves in high school. Mostly he sounded as though he hoped we would actually finish high school, and he seemed to be speaking as much to our parents as to us.

The first musical selection was called "In a Persian Market." I was embarrassed for the orchestra. Then Mr. Black introduced Mr. Folger from the Board of Education. Mr. Folger was big and red-faced, but what he said about education being a school for life made sense to me, and he told some funny stories to illustrate his advice. We gave him a big hand, and then Mr. Black got up and said he had a special treat for us. He said that the school was rarely fortunate enough to have a prodigy among its graduates, but that this year we had such a graduate. I looked down at my program again: The special treat was Hymie Silverstein, and he was going to play something called *Aubade Provençal*, by someone named Couperin, arranged by someone called Fritz Kreisler, and accompanied by the Foote School Orchestra under the direction of Mr. Shelley. Poor Hymie, I thought, what a buildup. Hymie walked onstage in a blue suit with his violin under his arm, and there was a mixture of giggles, whispers, and scattered applause. He looked completely at ease, as if the audience wasn't even there.

Mr. Shelley raised his baton and looked at Hymie. Hymie took out a white handkerchief, folded it carefully around the end of his violin, and tucked the violin under his chin. He lifted his bow and nodded to Mr. Shelley. The orchestra began to play; you could tell that they had struggled with this piece and they were still struggling. There was a short introduction that made us squirm in our seats, and then Hymie drew a single long note on his violin. The room was instantly silent; it made the hair on my neck stand up. He played a melody, his fingers vibrating on the strings. The orchestra came in behind him and seemed to have caught some skill by reflection. Hymie never looked up; he played as if he were singing the tune to himself. Suddenly the orchestra stopped and he played the theme again slowly and hauntingly. I heard a noise behind me; many women and a few men were holding handkerchiefs to their eyes. The two Russians sat towering above everyone else with tears rolling down their cheeks. Hymie played the melody faster and faster, turning it around different ways until his bow was flying. Suddenly he held a note on a long trill, and the orchestra came back in, repeated the theme with

Hymie's violin singing above them, and ended on three crashing chords. There was a second of silence, and then pandemonium. The applause was deafening, people were cheering in a dozen languages. Hymie bowed professionally and walked off the stage.

In a moment Mr. Black brought him back on. Hymie bowed again, walked over to Mr. Shelley and shook hands with him. Hymie shook hands with the first violinist of the orchestra, and Mr. Shelley asked the orchestra to stand. I clapped so hard my hands hurt. The applause died down, but the two Russians kept clapping slowly and powerfully, never changing their rhythm, and in a few moments the applause swelled to a roar again. Mr. Black smiled, threw up his hands, and brought Hymie out to the front of the stage with his arm around his shoulders. Hymie looked up at him and grinned, and for the first time he looked like the same kid who lived in the corner house at Third and South streets.

When the applause died down, Mr. Black introduced the teachers who were going to award prizes, but I wasn't listening. I sat there thinking about Hymie. All this time we had been making fun of him, stealing his coupons, and he belonged to a different world than we did. When he nodded to Mr. Shelley, it was as if he, not the teacher, were conducting the concert. I knew he wouldn't stay on South Street long.

Mrs. Barnes was droning about how important English and grammar were and then she gave a girl I didn't know a certificate and a big dictionary. I kept thinking about Hymie and how much he had accomplished and how little I had to show for my time. I was making up arguments to convince Tony that we shouldn't take Hymie's coupons anymore when suddenly I heard my name being called. "Solon Janus. Solon?" It was Mr. Feuter, up on the platform. I looked around, confused, and the kids near me laughed. "Get up there, jerk," some guy behind me said. I stood up, walked down the aisle, and climbed the steps to the stage carefully. Mr. Black shook hands with me, and then Mr. Feuter read a citation for excellence in mathematics and aptitude for science. He gave me a certificate and a narrow dark-green box. I was no Hymie; I felt myself turning red to the roots of my hair. I thanked him and stood in a daze with Hymie and the prizewinners for English, citizenship, and physical education while everyone applauded.

When I came back to my seat I opened the box. It was a slide rule, a real ivory and mahogany one. I was overcome; it was something I had wanted and never thought I would be able to afford. The rest of graduation went by in a fog. Mr. Black made another short speech, and we walked out to a recessional by Sir Arthur Sullivan. The musicians sounded glad that the whole thing was over.

Miss Geary gave us our diplomas and report cards in the hall outside, and when she handed me mine she gave me a hug and wished me good luck. I was surprised to see that I still had all A's, even in gym and geography. The parents and students were milling around in the halls and the yard outside. I kept looking for Cissie, but each time I saw a flash of yellow it was someone else. I did find Mr. Feuter. "I'm going to miss you, Sol," he said. "Don't forget to come back and visit."

"I will, Mr. Feuter. And thanks for all the help." A

moment later I caught sight of my mom waving to me. Georgios ran over, pushing between people. "Boy, we didn't know you were going to be up there. What'd they give you?" I showed him the slide rule; he looked disappointed. "What is it?"

"It's a slide rule. It's for doing calculations."

"Oh. I thought it might be a hunting knife because of the box shape."

My parents were also puzzled by the slide rule, but my father was impressed because it looked expensive. I handed him my report card. He took it out of the envelope, looked at it and nodded; that's the way it's supposed to be. Georgios read it from the side. "What a pain," he said. My mother kept hugging me.

When we got home, I couldn't wait to get out of my wool suit. I took out some cotton knickers from last summer and pulled them about three-quarters of the way up. That's all they would go. I called to my mom from the top of the stairs and showed her. She burst out laughing and called my father to see. It was the first time she had laughed like that since my beating. I clowned around to make her laugh some more, and then I put on a pair of corduroy winter knickers and came downstairs. "This afternoon we buy new," she said.

It took an hour to eat lunch, and on the way over to Goldstein's clothing store afterward we were still talking about graduation. My mother got tears in her eyes when she remembered Hymie's violin playing. *"Megalofeea,"* she said, "how do you say?"

"A genius."

"Neh, a little Jewish genius."

Three generations of Goldsteins worked in the clothing store, but my mother insisted on old Mr. Goldstein, who was bald and had to stand on a stool to check my collar. He wore blue suspenders and a striped shirt without a tie, and he pinched my cheek like the Greek aunts. I didn't like clothes shopping, but if you bought more than a pair of socks at Goldsteins's they gave you a baseball bat with their name on it. When Mr. Goldstein was measuring me I asked my mom if I could have long pants instead of knickers. She looked at me as if I were crazy. We bought new knickers, some polo shirts, lots of socks, and a new pair of sneakers. Everything was two sizes larger than my old clothes. At the end Mr. Goldstein gave me the biggest baseball bat he had. When I hefted it outside, it felt too small and light for me; I figured I could give it to Georgios.

CHAPTER 17

The club met at Harry's house that night. First everyone had to talk about graduation. Then because Harry and Mark were wearing new sneakers too, we spent ten minutes comparing brands. Eventually Tony called us to order and asked for old business. He was beginning to sound more like a real president. I asked how many coupons we had. He took the paper out of his pocket, unfolded it, and read, "As of Tuesday, June twenty-first, the club has collected twenty-nine thousand, nine hundred sixty-nine coupons for the *Clarion* Fabulous Fifty Contest."

Harry whistled. I couldn't believe my ears. I ran through a quick mental calculation, multiplying the days since Tony had showed me the ten thousand coupons by 400, which was less than a weekday total, but more than a Saturday or Sunday, and it came out about right. "We're a shoo-in," Mark said. "Nobody else could have that many."

"That's what you think," Tony said. "There are plenty of people who could have more than us."

Bobby looked skeptical. "That's an awful lot of coupons." I felt it was a good time to bring up my idea. "The contest ends on August fifteenth," I said. "If we collect just the Twelfth Street coupons from now until then we would have over forty-three thousand without any bonus papers or subscriptions."

"Why just from Twelfth Street?" Tony asked. "What about Hymie's route?"

"Well, I was thinking today at graduation when Hymie was playing. I was feeling bad about swiping his coupons."

Tony looked at me like I had a loose screw. "You gotta be kidding. What the hell difference does it make to Hymie if we swipe his coupons? He don't give a damn about the contest, he's too busy practicing his fiddle."

"I know what Sol means," Mark said. "I felt a little like that today."

"Like I said," Tony repeated, "what difference does it make? Hymie's customers wouldn't know what to do with the coupons if they did get them now. Besides, Hymie ain't gettin' hurt. He has the Russian goin' around with him, and we got the route wired."

I felt a twinge when Tony said that, the warning flick I got when something wasn't right on the street, but I couldn't think of a good answer. "I guess you're right," I said. "It was just a feeling I had." I couldn't shake off the feeling for the rest of the meeting. Maybe it was the hot, sticky night, but as Harry would say, something wasn't kosher. Tony noticed, because when we were walking home afterward he punched me on the arm and said, "Let's go down to Sonny's. My uncle gave me some money for graduation."

Sonny's was an oyster bar at Ninth and Christian in the Italian district. That night it was jammed. People overflowed out the door and along the sidewalk, most of them drinking near-beer and eating hard-shell crabs that had been boiled in pepper water. We got a couple of root beers and some crabs and walked through the alley away from the crowd. We sat down to eat in a corner below the high front steps of a house on Eighth Street. The sidewalk was still warm at eleven at night. Two men were sitting on the landing at the top of the steps drinking and talking. They didn't notice us, and we didn't pay any attention to them until Tony recognized one of their voices. "That's Joe Morello," he whispered in my ear. Morello was a ward boss, the father of one of the hoods shadowing Hymie. We picked the crabmeat out of the shells while Morello complained about the Philadelphia baseball teams. "But I'm gonna win that contest anyway," he said. "Even if there ain't no Philly teams in the Series."

"You mean the *Clarion* deal?" the other man said. "I didn't know you were in on that."

Morello gave a tremendous belch. "I'm in on everything."

"Sure, but that contest can't be nothin' like—"

"Like what?"

"Well, nothin', you know what I mean. I didn't think it was a big deal."

Morello belched again. "Well, maybe it ain't. But if anybody from the Strawberry Mansion mob is goin' on that trip, I'm damn well goin'. Hell, I got my boys workin' the whole ward. I got thirty-one thousand coupons now. Ain't nobody in the whole city gonna touch that." We looked at each other. Morello stood up. "C'mon, I'll call Sal and we'll play some pinochle. It's too hot to sleep."

The screen door banged shut behind them. "Thirty-one thousand! He's ahead of us already."

"I told you," Tony said. "We need every coupon we can get." We ate the rest of our crabs in silence. They didn't taste half as good after we heard about Morello's coupons.

I started helping my dad in the store the next day. He was a little less gruff than before graduation, but he still lost his temper if I did anything wrong. Some days I couldn't drop a nail without him yelling at me. It got to the place where collecting coupons in the early morning and playing ball with my friends in the evening were the only times I had any peace.

The next time I went up to Twelfth Street, Paul and Robert told me that they were going to camp in Maine for July and August. "We have two kids to do the route while we're away," Robert said. "They know about the coupons, so it'll be okay." They both congratulated me for graduating and winning the math prize. After we clipped the coupons, they took me over to Robert's garage to show me the gym he and his dad had built. They had an exercise mat like at school, a chinning bar, and a fancy barbell with weights you could change. "My dad got it because I was skinny," Robert said. "At first I could hardly do anything. Now I can do thirty push-ups, and I can press one hundred ten pounds."

I was sure that I was stronger than either of them. "Can I try?"

"Sure," Robert said. I bent over to pick up the barbell.

"Hold it! You'll hurt yourself if you lift it like that. Besides, you have to warm up first." He showed me some stretches—he was a lot better at them than I was—and then we tried the barbell. It was dead weight, heavier than I expected. We started at eighty pounds, and I passed them both with a shaky press of 125. "That's great without any practice," Robert said. "You could be really good if you trained. We can work out together after we come back from camp."

I could hardly move when I rolled out of bed the next day, but the stiffness went away and it got me thinking. A week later I was delivering a blowtorch to a construction site on Fitzwater Street, and I stopped and watched them pouring the concrete foundation. The foreman said they would be pouring for a week. That night I salvaged two empty fifty-pound nail cans, sawed out a pair of wooden circles that just fitted in the open ends, and drilled holes in them and the can ends for a piece of one-inch pipe. Then I cut two pieces of pipe a little longer than the cans, pushed them through the holes, and threaded female couplings on their inner ends. The next day I took the cans over to the building site in Georgios's wagon and asked the crew to fill them with concrete. Saturday morning I threaded a three-foot piece of pipe into the couplings and *presto*—my own barbell! It weighed 108 pounds on the store scale and I started working out with it the same day. My father thought I was nuts, but I could tell the difference in my hitting and throwing in two weeks.

You couldn't tell any difference in the National League right through July. The Pittsburgh Pirates held on to first place week after week, with the New York Giants chasing them, and the dependable Phillies in the cellar. The American League was more interesting. At the beginning of July the Cleveland Indians were still in first place, but the New York Yankees crept up on them steadily. On the twenty-first the Yanks beat them 7 to 1 and moved into the lead. That started a pennant race, with the Indians and the Yanks trading places. I calculated the percentage points on July 25 and the Yanks had .632 and the Indians had .640. Nothing bothered the A's, who stayed in last place the whole time.

July began the hot, sticky Philadelphia summer. I worked all day in the store, waiting for it to cool off in the evening so we could play ball. The other club members had overruled me about Hymie's coupons and two mornings a week I would collect his route. One morning I was clipping on Bainbridge Street at about five-thirty when I heard a splat on the sidewalk. "I see ya, ya dirty crook!" I looked up and there was a kid aiming spit at me from the edge of a roof. I gave him the finger and he gave it right back to me and disappeared. Big deal, I thought. Hymie was about two blocks ahead of me as usual, and I finished the route, had breakfast, and went to work in the store.

We were supposed to play a pickup baseball team on a vacant lot at Fourth and Fitzwater that night. I worked a little neatsfoot oil into the palm of my old glove after dinner. I started over to the game, and as I walked past an alley below Bainbridge two guys slipped out of it and grabbed my arms. "Don't try anything, Greeko." I recognized the smaller guy who had been tailing Hymie; it was like a red flag. I jerked out of his hold and twisted away from the other guy, who was much bigger. The skinny guy swung on me and I ducked it and punched him low in the stomach with all my might. He doubled over making sounds like he was going to vomit, and I started to bring one up to his jaw when there was a noise in my head like a giant bell clang and everything went black.

Everything was still black when I woke up. I was lying on the ground, and my head hurt like hell. I felt it and found a long tender welt right over the top. I started feeling the rest of me. Everything seemed okay except my left hand felt strange and I couldn't see much. I had a horrible thought: Maybe I was blind from the guy blackjacking me. I sat up, groped around, and realized that I still had my baseball glove on. There were some board walls on three sides and a door in front. I pushed the door open; it was dark but I could see! I was so excited to find that I wasn't blind that I struggled to my feet and hit the sore top of my head on the roof of the shed. I was in somebody's backyard off the alley. I crept home, feeling dizzy and like I had to throw up. Somehow I managed to get to bed without my parents knowing what happened. I told Tony the next day, but the Mafia had already sent him a message. They had finally figured out our system, and my welt was their announcement that we weren't going to get any more of Hymie's coupons.

CHAPTER 18

On August 2 we had the next-to-the-last club meeting before the end of the *Clarion* contest on the fifteenth. We were all in Harry's kitchen at seven o'clock. I expected Tony to give us a big pep talk about collecting coupons right to the end of the contest, but we just sat around drinking cream sodas and eating potato chips, talking about nothing in particular. "Did it hurt?" Mark asked me without any warning.

"Yeah. It still hurts sometimes, but it's mostly better. I have a hard head." Tony looked at me as if he were trying to see through my hair. He stood up and called the meeting to order. "Old business," he announced.

"How many coupons do we have?" Bobby asked.

Tony took out his slip of paper. "As of today we got forty-three thousand, one hundred eleven coupons."

"Is that enough to win?"

Tony looked evasive. "It ain't so easy, like I said. I heard that the Polish-American Guild in Manayunk has fifty thousand, and some synagogue in Germantown—"

"Dammit, Ammanati, cut the crap!" Mark burst out. "It ain't the Poles and it ain't the Jews, it's the lousy Mafia and everybody knows it." He stood up, towering over Tony threateningly. "Now what's the story, do we have enough to win or don't we?"

I had never seen Mark lose his temper before. Tony

looked around the circle of club members and seemed to wilt. "I didn't mean nothin' personal. Okay, if you mean do we have enough to be first, we don't. There are some . . . guys that have more. They just got too big an organization."

"But do we have enough to be in the top fifty?"

I had been figuring on a scrap of paper. "We should have about forty-five thousand, five hundred by the end of the contest."

Tony looked frightened. "Look, I don't know. It's—I can't say, I think we got enough. It ain't my fault, in fact that's what I wanted to talk about. We gotta move the coupons; they're not safe at my house anymore."

"How come?" Bobby asked.

"Well, there's too many. And my folks might wanta use the trunk," he finished weakly.

We all looked at each other. "Sure, they might," Mark said. "Okay, where can we keep 'em?"

"Here," Harry said. "We have plenty of room in the cellar, and we got all kinds of boxes and cans from the store."

"How soon do we have to move them?" Bobby asked.

"The sooner we get 'em out of my house the better," Tony said.

"Okay, let's move them tonight," I said. "We can carry most of them in Georgio's wagon and divide up the rest between us. Right now."

Tony shrugged. "Moved and seconded?" I made a motion, Mark seconded it, and we adjourned the meeting.

Everyone seemed relieved to have something to do. We took a couple of big cartons from Harry's, picked up the wagon at my house, and filled the cartons in the areaway behind Tony's basement door. We wrapped the rest in newspaper and each of us carried two bundles. At first I was nervous, but the whole thing went smoothly. We stored everything in Harry's cellar and stacked a lot of other cartons in front of them. If we didn't know where they were, we would have had a hard time finding them ourselves.

The next morning I was building drawers for machine screws out of cheese boxes when Bobby walked into the store. "What's new, Bobby?"

"Nothin' much. That was funny about Tony last night."

"I guess he's in the middle a little bit."

He looked around to see where my father was. "I got a message for you." He took an envelope out of his pocket. "Go ahead, read it."

I tore it open. It was a note from Cissie. She said she was sorry I had gotten hurt again, and she had missed me this summer. She wanted to wish me good luck in high school. That's how the note was signed: "Best of luck, Cissie." I still thought about her every night, but I hadn't been able to see her in the daytime after school ended. Seeing her name brought my feelings back and I felt myself coloring. "I was wondering if you were busy tonight," Bobby said.

"Nope. My head still doesn't feel right when I play ball. Why?"

"I have to take some clothes and stuff down to Cissie's house. I thought you could help me carry it."

"Sure, why not?" Because it was in the heart of Irish town, that was why not. That was why I didn't go down to see Cissie myself, because the streets were full of mick gangs waiting to pounce on anyone who didn't look Irish and beat the crap out of him. That was what they did for amusement on summer nights, and since a lot of the cops were Irish, the gangs got away with it.

"Great. Come over to my house around seven o'clock."

"Okay." I was trying so hard to sound like I wasn't worried about the gangs that I never thought about what it would be like to see Cissie again.

When I got to Bobby's house, he was sitting on the front steps surrounded by younger brothers and sisters. His parents were always ahead of me; every time I got the names of their kids straight, they had another one. Dolores was my favorite that year. She was five, and her red hair and freckles made her look like a little version of Cissie. Bobby lifted her off his lap. "Okay, toots, play with Uncle Sol. I'll get the stuff," he said to me. "It's clothes for my Aunt Grace to fix."

I sat down on the step and Dolores climbed onto my lap. A little boy in diapers pulled himself up to my knee and gummed my knickers. "Get down, Jimmy," Dolores said. He sat down and untied my shoelace. Dolores cuddled against me and smiled into my eyes. "I really like you, Sol."

"That's nice, Dolores, I like you too."

She poked a finger into my shirt pocket and smiled up at me again. "You have any candy?" she whispered.

"Cut it out, brat," Bobby said. "You know you're not supposed to ask people for presents."

"I was just asking if he had any," she said sulkily.

"Never mind, lay off or I'll tell Mom." He handed me a bundle of clothes, and we started down Third Street. "Cissie lives on Sauter, doesn't she?" I asked.

"Two forty-one. You been down there?"

"Nope."

"It ain't bad. Nicer than our block."

"What's her father do?"

"I think he works for a tugboat company, somethin' like that."

"Who're the clothes for?"

"My aunt's gonna fix them up for her kids. We trade them back and forth, depending on who fits what."

I couldn't imagine having seven brothers and sisters. "You like having such a big family?"

Bobby shrugged. "It's okay. I didn't have much to say about it."

We both laughed. "What's so funny now, fellas?" a voice said behind us.

We turned around. It was the mick advance guard, two big red-faced guys who looked like they had been into the sauce for a while. "Nothin'," Bobby said.

"We don't want to miss a joke, boy, do we now?"

"It wasn't a joke."

"Wasn't it, then?" He plucked at the pile of clothes in my arms. "And what might be these handsome packets you're carrying?"

"Clothes for my Aunt Grace. Grace Nolan. From Sauter Street."

"That's Big Mike's wife," the other one said. "Are you related to that fine family?"

"I said she's my aunt. My father is her brother."

"Well, and you're the lucky one. And what about this eye-talian-lookin' fella, is he related too?"

"I'm Greek," I said.

"He's my friend Sol Janus. We're in a club together."

"And so are we. It's a shame you haven't got enough

good Irish folk to fill up your club with."

"C'mon, Tim, I'm thirsty," the second one said.

"Right then, boys, we just wanted to make sure that you're travelin' safely."

Sure you did, you big goon, I thought. They must have had some kind of high sign, because the next two groups we passed didn't pay any attention to us. "Here it is," Bobby said. We climbed the steps of a tall brick row house. He walked in without knocking and I followed along.

"Aren't you the fine ones!" Mrs. Nolan looked up from a sewing machine when we came into the kitchen. "Just let me finish this seam, darlings." She pedaled the machine with smooth, even strokes and guided the fabric under the needle rapidly. There were piles of clothes like the ones we carried strewn over the big kitchen table. "There!" Mrs. Nolan held up a rebuilt blouse. "You'd think they could stop growing if they put their minds to it. Who's your friend? All I have is some oatmeal cookies and tea, but I'm sure they'll do you a world of good." She was moving while she talked, striking a match on her skirt and lighting the stove burner with a great whoosh, the way my father told us we should never do it because you could have an explosion. "This is my friend Sol Janus, Aunt Grace."

"Sol, is it? It's a bit of a kikey-sounding name, but any friend of yours is a friend of mine, and I'm grateful for the help." She put a kettle on the stove, swept one of the clothes piles onto the floor, and set out cups and saucers. "Sol is Greek, Aunt Grace."

"Greek! Well, that's different anyhow. Janus is your last, Mr. Sol?"

"Yes. Solon Demetrios Janus."

She stopped measuring the tea and looked at me hard. "What a mouthful. I believe I've heard a bit about you. A smart one, isn't that right?"

"He won the mathematics prize at school," Bobby said.

"Lord save us. You'll probably be goin' to college like the O'Malley boy did a few years back. I don't believe his parents ever saw him again. He went to college somewhere and went straight on to California. Can you imagine, runnin' off like that and not a bit of use to his family? He might as well have gone back to the old country. You wouldn't believe the things they tell about the university in Dublin, for that matter. A regular zoo. Here, try that." She filled the teacups and put down a plate of cookies. I caught a glimpse of Cissie in her cheekbones and the tilt of her nose. "And what line of work would your father be in, Mr. Janus?"

"He has a hardware store, ma'am. On South Street near Third."

"Well, it could be worse. We're in the shipping ourselves. Mr. Nolan, that is. What do you think of those cookies?"

"They're delicious, Mrs. Nolan."

"Sure, I have to admit it. I eat too many of them myself."

I kept looking around for Cissie while we ate, but she was nowhere in sight. When we finished Mrs. Nolan took the cups away, and we got up to leave. "Thank you for carrying my bundle, young Mr. Janus, and come back again. I'll have some fine corned beef for you. I'll bet the Greeks don't make that."

"No, ma'am, they don't. Thank you very much."

"Thanks, Aunt Grace," Bobby said.

"Is that all there is for it?"

He went over and gave her a big hug and kiss. I could see that he was embarrassed. "That's better," Mrs. Nolan said. "You're not so big as all that." We went out the door to the dark hall. I was really disappointed. We were almost at the front door when Cissie's voice said, "Hello, Sol."

CHAPTER 19

The hair on the back of my neck stood up at the sound of her voice. I turned around; she was sitting near the bottom of the stairs, and I could just make out her mischievous smile. "I thought you weren't home."

"I was just waiting until my mum was finished with you. Let's go for a walk."

"Okay." Very polished, very grown-up. I looked around for Bobby, but he had magically disappeared. We went out the front door and down the steps. It was dusky dark. The air was as warm and thick as syrup; I felt that I was slowly swimming through it. We walked down Sauter to Third and turned south on Third Street. Cissie seemed to know where she was going, and I swam along beside her, content to brush against her bare arm for the rest of my life. At the corner of League Street she linked her little finger in mine, and a while after that we were holding hands. Holding hands! Did I wash my hands before I left home? I felt each one of her fingers against mine, gently pressed against each little knuckle. Every part of her hand felt smooth, beautiful, small, and perfect.

At Washington Street we walked along the park next to the Washington Elementary School. The park had an iron fence around it that they locked at night, but Cissie led me to a place where the bushes grew through the fence and overhung the sidewalk. "Feel for the space," she said. I tested the bars one by one and found two that had been bent apart enough for a person to squeeze through. Cissie slipped between them easily, but I had to scrape and push, sliding up and down to get the wider parts of me through the middle of the gap. I felt a belt loop catch and tear, but I didn't care at all.

"This way," Cissie whispered, and I followed her along a narrow but well-worn path through the bushes. Suddenly she stopped and squeezed my hand. "Oops," she whispered. I followed her glance to the couple lying on the grass side by side. She pulled my hand and we detoured around them and found another path that led to an empty bench. I was full of confused feelings. Cissie seemed so pure, but she wasn't embarrassed by the lovemakers at all. "There," she said, settling back against the bench. "Now, talk to me. I want to hear all about you."

She was still holding my hand, and all I could think about was her skin and her closeness. "Where should I start?"

"Start with this summer. I missed you. Did you miss me?"

"Of course I missed you. I thought about you every night."

"Did you really? I love that. I was so proud of you at graduation."

"I looked for you afterward, but every time I saw a yellow dress it was someone else."

"What did you do this summer?"

I told her about working in the store and my father and baseball, and after a while I put her hand down. I was proud of myself for letting go of it. Of course by that time we were half facing each other and our knees were touching, and my eyes were used to the dark and I could see the curves of her breasts against her dress. I was tempted to tell her about the coupons—maybe Bobby had—but I didn't. I told her about Paul and Robert and how beautiful their houses were, and somehow we came around to my father again and I told her about my beating. I had never felt so strange and confused; we kept getting sadder and sadder and more and more excited at the same time. Cissie was close to tears. "Oh," she said, "that's the saddest thing I've ever heard in my life." The next second we were in each others' arms. "Oh Cissie," I heard myself saying, "I love you."

"I love you too. Isn't it wonderful?"

I pulled apart a little and took her face in my hands. It was like holding an icon. I started kissing at one side of her cheek, and I kissed her whole face, one kiss at a time, until there wasn't anything else in the world but that place.

After a while we both sat back and took a breath. "Oh," Cissie sighed, "this must be what they write stories about." She leaned back against my arm and looked up at the stars. We kissed again and this time we touched tongues right away and everything became more insistent. I couldn't hold her tight enough. "Sol," she gasped, "I won't have any breath left if you squeeze me like that."

I kissed her again. "You're so beautiful," I said.

"So are you." She turned to me and kissed me again while the stars turned slowly above us. It was the most wonderful night of my life, and no one could ever take it away from me.

CHAPTER 20

My dreams changed after that night. For many weeks I dreamed of holding Cissie close to me, keeping her safe from harm. Bobby knew how we were right away. He carried notes between me and Cissie almost every day until the end of summer.

Business in the store was slow during August, and the days seemed to drag by while we waited for the end of the contest. On Sunday, August 14, the *Clarion* printed a bonus of ten coupons in every copy of the paper because it was the last day. That night we had a special club meeting to make a final count and pack up the coupons. Tony and I were appointed to deliver them to the *Clarion* Monday morning. Mark had persuaded his cousin Joe to pick us up in his delivery truck at the end of his route and give us a ride to the *Clarion* building on Broad Street. It took a couple of hours to tie up the bundles and stack them neatly in cartons. The grand total was 46,523 coupons. "I never thought we'd get that many," Bobby said.

"Remember the beginning of the contest?" I asked.

"Sure, I thought of it," Tony said.

"Well, we have forty-six thousand, three hundred fifty-six more coupons than if we had saved the one in the paper every day."

"Is that right?" Harry said. "That really tickles my funny bone. I'm almost gonna miss getting up early in the morning."

I kept waking up that night the way I did the first night of the contest. Joe was supposed to meet us at Harry's house around six-thirty. I trotted over there and met Tony and Mark coming around the corner. "Good timing, sport," Tony said. Bob and Harry were already waiting for us. We just had time to open the cellar doors and carry the cartons up to the sidewalk before Joe pulled up in his big chain-drive Keystone truck. I thought I was in pretty good shape, but Joe had the muscles of a blacksmith. He picked up our cartons as though they were empty and slung them in the back of the truck. "Let's go, fellas, I gotta get back for the two-star edition."

We all shook hands. "Good luck, you guys," Harry said. "Yeah, good luck," Bobby and Mark echoed. They looked wistful. Tony and I climbed into the opensided cab and Joe started down Lombard toward Broad Street. I leaned out and waved back at the guys. I had never ridden in a truck cab before, and while I had seen the controls many times, I wasn't sure how they were used. I watched Joe shift gears with practiced ease. You could feel every cobblestone in the street through the solid rubber tires. "Runs like silk when she's empty, don't she," he said proudly.

"She sure does."

"How many coupons you guys got?"

"Forty-six thousand and some," Tony said.

"Is that right? That sounds pretty good."

"Have you heard any other totals?" I asked.

"There's lots of stories about fifty thousand, but you

can't believe that crap. We been hearing stuff like that since the beginning of the contest." He downshifted and turned right on Broad Street. There was very little traffic as we drove north, around City Hall, and headed toward the *Clarion* building at Broad and Callowhill. Suddenly Joe braked and peered ahead. "What the hell—?" Starting at Race Street the northbound lanes were choked with standing automobiles. We were still four blocks from the *Clarion*. "Dammit, how am I supposed to get through that?" Joe muttered. He turned right, detoured up Thirteenth Street, and swung back toward Broad Street at Spring Garden, two blocks above the newspaper. When we reached the intersection the scene was exactly the same as it was to the south. "This looks like the damn Armistice," Joe said. "Okay, you buggers." He gunned the truck's engine and began to weave between the cars blocking the intersection. I could see cartons and bags of coupons in every car. "Holy Mother," Tony said. "Who would've thought."

"Don't give me any crap!" Joe yelled at a driver who refused to back up and let him cross Broad Street. "I'll push you right into the damn sidewalk!" The man reluctantly gave way, and Joe manhandled the truck onto Fifteenth Street and down to the loading dock of the *Clarion*. "Dumb bastards, clogging up the intersections like that. C'mon, boys, I'll give you a hand with them boxes." He picked up two of the four cartons. Tony and I followed him through a maze of corridors, each of us carrying one of the heavy cartons of coupons. We struggled up a flight of stairs and came out in the vast front lobby of the *Clarion*.

There were two desks near the marble back wall with

men sitting behind them recording totals, and two crews of boys with carts to carry the coupons to wherever they stored them. In front of each desk was a line of people stretching all the way across the lobby, out the front doors of the building, and up or down Broad Street. Everyone had boxes or bags full of coupons. At seven o'clock in the morning! Joe walked over to one of the desks, talked to the man behind it for a moment, and beckoned to us. Tony turned to me. "We forgot to choose! Whose name should we use?"

"Yours. You're the president, and we can change it later if we have to."

"We'll take you right now, boys." The man behind the desk smiled. Two or three people waiting glared at us. "Who do they think they are?" a fat man who was next in line said.

"They're orphans," Joe said. "Special guests of the paper. Any problems?" His muscles bulged ominously.

"No, no, just asking," the fat man said. "I'm sorry, boys." I tried to look like an orphan. "How many coupons do you have, boys?" the clerk asked. Tony handed him a slip with the total written on it. "Forty-six thousand, five hundred and twenty-three," the man intoned as he wrote it down. "Not bad, boys."

"Did you hear that?" the fat man asked the man behind him. "Forty-six thousand! They must have had the whole orphanage collecting. You know how hard I had to work to get nine thousand?"

"What name do you want these under?" the clerk asked.

"Tony Ammanati." Tony spelled it out for him.

"There you are." The clerk handed Tony a receipt. "Don't lose it. Good luck, boys." We could hear the news of our total traveling along the line as we followed Joe to the stairs. "They'll be there all day," he said. "Serves 'em right, screwing up traffic like that."

Tuesday morning's *Clarion* had a front-page article about the contest, with pictures of the cars taken from the roof of the newspaper building. Joe was right, it was the biggest traffic jam since the Armistice. The article said that the response to the contest had been so overwhelming that it would take two weeks to verify the coupon counts. The winners would be announced on September 1.

And what about the great Philadelphia baseball teams that were supposed to win the pennants and be the focus of all this excitement? You can probably guess. On August 15, the last day of the Fabulous Fifty contest, the Cleveland Indians lost to the Chicago White Sox 4 to 1 and dropped into second place. That put the New York Yankees into first place in the American League and left the Philadelphia Athletics in last place. In the National League the Pittsburgh Pirates held a slim lead over the New York Giants with a .624 win percentage, and down in the cellar, with a mighty .366, were the Phillies. We could have had the basement World Series in Philadelphia.

I was so used to clipping the coupon on the front page of the *Clarion* that the paper looked strange without it. The next morning I was sweeping the sidewalk in front of the store when Hymie walked by. He gave me a big smile. "What's new, Hymie?"

"Nothing much, practicing, getting ready for school. Hey, doesn't the paper look funny without—"

"A coupon in it?"

"I was going to say a hole." That seemed terribly funny, and we both cracked up. I realized what a relief it was not to be stealing coupons. "I hear you're going to Central," he said. "When do you start?"

"September fifth. How about you?"

"On the twelfth. I got a scholarship to the Philadelphia Music Academy."

"Gee, congratulations. You were really terrific at graduation."

"Thanks, Sol. I'll have to play for you sometime, just private."

"That would be great." He walked off whistling. Well, what the hell, I thought, it might be great. I was just opening the store when Mr. Persichetti, the mailman, came by. "Hello there, Sol. I got a nice letter from the old country for your ma, some hardware catalogs for your dad, and a postcard for you. Color picture and everything." I was surprised; there was never mail for me. I took the card up to my room. It had a picture of a dock with some fishing boats and a lot of dark green trees behind them. On the back was printed *Picturesque Lobster Boats Unloading at Point of Pines, Maine.* The postmark was Saturday, August 13. "Dear Sol: Our camp had a clambake on the beach near here today. It was great, we had lobster and steamed clams and corn on the cob. We're having a terrific summer. I learned to play tennis and shoot a .22 rifle. Robert and I both passed our swimming test. Hope you're having a good summer too. See you on the 21st. Best regards, Paul."

I read it three or four times. The only familiar thing was corn on the cob. I had never eaten lobster or clams, I had never held a tennis racket, and I had never shot a rifle. I had pulled the trigger on my father's revolver once after unloading the cartridges, and worried for weeks that he would find out about it. I could stay afloat in the water and flail along, but I was sure that Paul and Robert were learning the Australian Crawl like the swimmers in newspaper pictures. I promised myself that I would practice my weights and baseball all I could in the few days before they came home.

Time seemed to move even slower after we delivered our coupons than before. At the next club meeting we had very little to talk about. The other guys were all excited about the South Philly High football team, but I couldn't get interested in that. The best thing that happened that week was that I had another night with Cissie. We went back to Washington Park, and it was even better than the first time because we could take time to talk. I thought that I could talk to her for hours and make love to her for days. Neither of us mentioned how close it was to the beginning of school. We knew it would be different with us in separate high schools. It would be doubly different for me because there were no girls at Central High. The college preparatory girls in Philadelphia went to Girls' High. When Harry asked me if Central had dances with them, Tony cracked up. "Girls' High! They're the ugliest girls in the whole city. They're all flat-chested four-eyes or big fat brains." I thought he didn't know what he was talking about, but later on when I met them it turned out he wasn't far wrong.

CHAPTER 21

We were eating dinner on the evening of the twenty-second when the telephone rang. It was Paul Fraser; he had come home on Sunday, and could I come over that evening? I told him sure, and he said he'd call Robert and we could talk. When I rang his doorbell I heard him pounding down the stairs. "I'll get it," he called. Mr. and Mrs. Fraser were sitting in the living room reading the papers. Mr. Fraser put down his pipe and shook hands with me. "Hello, Sol. You seem to have grown a lot since last spring."

"Yes, sir, I can't help it."

Mrs. Fraser laughed her tinkly laugh. She looked prettier than ever in a little white summer dress with one leg tucked up under her. I still had trouble thinking of her as Paul's mother. "It's nice to see you back, Sol," she said. "Did you have a nice summer?"

"Yes, ma'am."

"Well, I'm glad." She gave me an impish smile. I felt uncomfortable around her, attracted and worried at the same time. Just then Robert came in and in a few minutes we escaped to Paul's room. They both looked tanned and fit. "Your camp sounds great," I said.

"It was mostly okay," Paul said. "Some of the kids were a pain in the ass."

"Not to mention some of the counselors," Robert added.

"It's good to be home. I was getting pretty sick of oatmeal for breakfast every day."

"And cold showers," Paul said.

"And blackflies. Have you ever been anywhere where they had blackflies?"

"Are they like those big Jersey horseflies?"

"Oh no, you can't swat these guys. They're real tiny, the Indians up there used to call them no-see-ums. They eat you alive, and you can't do a thing about it. They come out in clouds after the rain, and there are millions of them."

I was feeling better and better to find out that camp wasn't so great. We lounged on the bed and ate some of Velma's cookies, and they told me about the rifle range and their canoe trip. "What about you?" Paul asked.

"I didn't do much," I said. I wasn't going to tell them about Cissie. "Worked in the store, played ball, collected coupons—"

"Coupons—I forgot all about them," Robert said. "What happened with the contest?"

"We don't know. They're supposed to publish the winners on September first." I told them about our 46,000 coupons, and the end of the contest, and my run-in with the Mafia.

"That's really scary," Paul said, looking at my head.

"Yeah," Robert echoed. "I would have peed in my pants."

"Well, I feel okay now, so I guess it wasn't so bad. I've been working out with a barbell I made."

"Well, now you can work out with us. You're gonna love Central."

I was starting to believe that. I hoped that looking forward to high school would carry me through the *Clarion* announcement, but it was no match for an August heat wave. By midweek I was as crabby as my dad, snapping at Georgios and sweating all the time. We went through a case of flypaper in two days. Ten minutes after you hung a strip up it would be covered with buzzing flies. They flew straight into the store from the piles of horse manure in the street; I hated them.

Rumors about the Fabulous Fifty contest were everywhere. We heard that a North Philly gang had hijacked two *Clarion* delivery trucks and turned in 60,000 coupons. There was another story about a guy who forged a printing plate and made 50,000 fakes. It seems strange now that people would go to so much trouble for baseball tickets, but it meant a whole week of deluxe travel and entertainment, and that was a big prize in 1921.

Believe it or not, I overslept on September first. I jumped out of bed at eight o'clock and ran downstairs; did any of the club members call? No, no one, my mom said. Maybe they were waiting to publish the results in the late edition. At eight-thirty Tony came over and told me that the *Clarion* wasn't able to meet the deadline. There was a notice on the front page from the contest director explaining that their tabulators were still counting day and night, and they hoped to have the totals by September third. Later I heard that some of the *Clarion* newsstands downtown had been turned over by angry crowds.

In a way the late results took a little of the tension out of waiting. I just worked in the store for the next two days and tried to avoid people. Monday was going to be my first day of high school. It was beginning to feel more important to me than the Fabulous Fifty contest, but Saturday morning I woke up at the crack of dawn. I dressed and slipped downstairs, and I wasn't surprised when Tony trotted around the corner of Third Street. Two minutes later Mark and Bobby appeared, and five minutes after that Harry walked up with a sheepish grin on his face. When Hymie came along to pick up his papers we were waiting for him, and we walked to the dropoff together. There were a dozen other people already at the corner, looking up the street for Joe Kolaks's truck. "He's late," somebody said. "I bet they don't have them today either."

"No he's not." Hymie pulled up his sleeve and looked at his wristwatch. "Joe is always on time." He noticed me looking at the watch. "It was my graduation present. I wanted a new bow, but it was too expensive." Just then Joe's truck came screeching around the corner like a race car. In fact, there were cars chasing him just like in a race, with people yelling that they wanted to buy papers. Joe didn't pay any attention to them; he just pulled up to the curb, slung Hymie's bundle of *Clarion*s onto the sidewalk with one hand, shifted gears, and was off again. "Hey!" Mark yelled after him, "Hey, Joe! Did we win?" Joe waved out the side and stepped on it. The cars kept chasing him like they were loony.

By that time there were about fifty people from Hymie's route waiting for their papers. We helped untie the bundle and handed papers to people for him. "Dammit," one man said, "I knew it was fixed." He threw his paper on the ground and walked away. I picked it up and the club gathered around me. The giant headline was there again— THE FABULOUS FIFTY!—and under it, taking up the whole front page and surrounded by the *Clarion*'s entire stock of stars and rockets, was the list of fifty names. I started reading through it with the other guys breathing over my shoulders. Nothing, nothing, nothing . . . then I found it: *Number 17, Tony Ammanati.* A triumphant shriek went up from the five of us, and everyone standing on Hymie Silverstein's corner knew what the yelling was about. "Which one of them? A cousin, maybe?" In five minutes the news was all over South Street.

On page two of the *Clarion* they asked the winners to contact the paper and show their receipts. The article explained that all the travel arrangements would be made by the Fabulous Fifty staff before the World Series began in October. Tony would have to be excused from school, we realized. The decision that Tony would be the one to go was as simple as that; we never even chose up. The list of extra prizes filled page three from top to bottom. There were many more than when the contest started. Bobby read through it slowly, smiling. I think that was the first time he was really glad we had done it.

The next day the Ammanati house was a tourist attraction, like Independence Hall. People from all over South Philadelphia walked by it, gesturing and talking in Italian, Yiddish, Polish, and Russian. The next few weeks our store even picked up some business when the story of the club got around. It was funny, during the contest I was worried about people finding out about us, but after we won nobody seemed to mind that we had stolen most of our coupons. In fact, some people almost seemed proud that we had won with their coupons. My father shrugged when people told him how clever we were, but my mother hugged me a dozen times for no reason.

CHAPTER 22

Monday was my first day at Central High. I took the trolley car to Broad and Green streets full of apprehension. The trolley cost seven cents a trip, and the night before my father had showed me a sheet of paper filled with rows and columns of sevens. He had figured out that at 14 cents a day, 70 cents a week, transportation to Broad and Green streets for the school year added up to $27.30. He didn't like it at all.

When we arrived at school, there was a whole list of things to be done. It felt very grown-up and different. After we registered and were directed to our homerooms, each incoming freshman was given a thick manila envelope with his name on it and told to read through the papers inside. On top of the pile was a letter from the principal:

Dear Mr. Janus: (Me!)

On behalf of the faculty of The Central High School of Philadelphia, I would like to welcome you to the class of 1925. You will doubtless be aware that your outstanding academic performance so far has gained you admission to an elite institution, and to a class of like-minded fellows. We expect that you will continue to maintain high standards during your four years at Central High, and we trust that those years will prove to be happy and productive ones for you. It is also our hope, nay, our expectation, that after graduation you will go on to distinguish yourself and contribute to the splendid record of your predecessor alumni.

This letter of welcome is accompanied by some information that I feel sure will prove useful to you during your freshman year. Please feel free to call upon me at any time if I may be of help to you. With very best regards, I am

> *Yours very truly,*
> *Dana Farnsworth, Ph.D.,*
> *Principal*

I still have that letter. The second page was a map of Central High. It was huge and complicated; it looked as if the whole Foote School would fit in the gymnasium. In the beginning everything about Central seemed wonderful and complicated. It was like a scary candy store, but after a while I got used to it.

The major distraction during my first month of high school was baseball. Now that we had won the Fabulous Fifty contest I began to follow the games even more closely. Me and everyone else. As though they knew people were watching, the New York teams really began to get on the ball. On September first the Yankees increased their lead in the American League by beating the Washington Senators 9 to 3, and on Friday the ninth they came to Philadelphia and showed the A's what baseball was all about. The final score was Yankees 14, Athletics 5, and the Yanks knocked three of Connie Mack's pitchers out of the box. The most exciting thing was that Babe Ruth hit his 54th home run of the season in that game. He tied his own world record from the year before, and his homer was the longest ball ever hit in Shibe Park. "Just wait, I'm gonna get his autograph when I meet him," Tony said at the next club meeting.

"How do you know you'll meet him?" Harry asked.

"I will, you wait and see." I envied him a lot when he said that. We should have chosen up, I thought.

The same day that the Yanks beat the A's, the New York Giants whittled the Pittsburgh Pirates' lead in the National League down to nothing. That was the first time I ever saw averages printed out to four places: Pittsburgh .6060, New York .6053. On the eleventh they beat the Brooklyn Robins 11 to 3 and jumped into the National League lead.

Babe Ruth broke his home run record on Thursday, September 15, helping the Yanks sweep a doubleheader over the St. Louis Browns. It would have been a happy day for me, except that after school I came around the corner of Third Street and bumped right into Cissie. "Ah, hi, Cissie," was all I could manage.

"Hi, Sol. How is Central?" She smiled at me. She looked gorgeous.

"It's neat. I mean it's—different. It's nice to see you."

"It's nice to see you too." God, you're beautiful, I wanted to say, I want to go back to that night. I had expected to be embarrassed when I met her, and I thought that she'd be embarrassed too. She wasn't at all. "Do you have good teachers?" I heard myself asking.

"All right, I guess. My typing teacher is nice looking. Do you?"

"They're okay. No one I like especially." We sounded like a couple of strangers. I realized that she was looking over my shoulder. "Well, I have to go now," she said.

"I really like seeing you again."

"It's nice to see you too," she said again. "See you soon."

I turned and watched her. When she came to the next corner, two other girls and three boys met her. "Hi, Cissie!" they called, and all of them started chattering together. I stood there like I was in the middle of a vacant lot. It wasn't that she wasn't nice or anything, I told myself. She was perfectly polite, and she did say see you again. I started walking automatically. I felt much worse than if we had had a fight. When I got home I went straight up to my room and lay down on the bed. I felt so rotten and locked up I couldn't even cry.

For the next two weeks I concentrated on school, baseball, and hardware so I wouldn't think about Cissie. There was plenty of homework during the week, and I worked long hours in the store on the weekends. I did crazy things, like sorting all the machine screws and making new partitions for the drawers we kept them in. Stove bolts, carriage bolts, National Coarse and National Fine, 6-32, 8-32, 10-24, ¼-20, you could get lost in that stuff and not think about anything else for hours. After I finished sorting I varnished all the drawer fronts. My father couldn't figure it out.

The Giants still had a few games to play, but they sewed up the National League pennant by beating the Pittsburgh Pirates 5 to 0 on September 16. On the twenty-sixth the *Clarion* ran a picture of the new baseball commissioner, Judge Kenesaw Mountain Landis, watching his secretary toss a coin to decide where the first game would be played. Ban Johnson, the American League president, called heads, and the coin fell tails. John Heydler, president of the National League, decided that the opener would be played at the National League team's home field. Tickets would be six dollars for the boxes, four and five dollars for reserved seats, and a buck for the bleachers. By the end of September the Yanks and the Giants were solidly ahead, and it looked like those seats would be at the New York Polo Grounds, which was home for both teams. The first Subway Series, the papers called it.

By the end of September we also knew more about the Fabulous Fifty. The *Clarion* published the coupon totals and articles about the top ten winners. Number one was a little old lady named Markevich from Germantown who turned in sixty-two thousand coupons. Sixty-two thousand! No one else was even close. She had white hair and a shawl around her shoulders, and she looked as if she would blow away in a breeze. The article told how she liked to garden and bake pies. The next day we found out she ran the biggest numbers game in the city. She had inherited it from her brother, who was knifed when he tried to shake down a ward boss in Strawberry Mansion. There were fifteen mafiosi between her and us, but below number twenty-five the totals went down fast, and the last man on the list had only eight thousand coupons.

Tony had a pile of letters and instructions from the *Clarion*. The Fabulous Fifty train would leave for New York on Tuesday, October 4, the day before the first game. Tony acted more and more nervous as the day came closer. Sunday night he asked me if I would go to the *Clarion* building with him Tuesday morning. His father couldn't leave his business and his mother was too scared to go. I told him sure, if he could get me out of classes. I didn't think he could, but he had a lawyer friend of his father send a note to the principal of Central about me and the club, and darned if I didn't get a pass for Tuesday morning from the office. It turned out that Dr. Farnsworth was a baseball fan like everyone else.

CHAPTER 23

Monday night I told my mom I was going to the *Clarion* in the morning with Tony, and she pressed my suit and a shirt. She got up to make me breakfast, and when I came downstairs she gave me a hug and slipped a little packet of money into my hand. She had been doing that since I started Central. *"Efkharisto,* Momma."

"Parakalo." She reached up and patted my hair. *"Oraios."*

I laughed. "I wish I was handsome. Don't worry, I'll see you this afternoon."

It was a crisp morning with a few high clouds in a blue sky—the kind of fall day that Philadelphians waited for all summer so they could brag about it. I had my schoolbooks, because I was going on to school from the newspaper. Tony was standing outside his house with an old leather suitcase when I walked up. I was feeling flush because my mother had given me six dollars and change. "Look at this," Tony said. He opened his wallet and showed me five new five-dollar bills. "How about that? My old man wanted me to have some spending money. That's the most he ever gave me."

We took a trolley to Thirteenth Street and transferred to a northbound car. At Callowhill we got off and walked over to Broad Street. "Wow, look at that!" Tony said as we reached the corner. The front of the *Clarion* building was draped in red, white, and blue bunting two stories high. There was a red carpet cordoned off with velvet ropes from the front door down to the curb, and the sidewalk was packed solid with people on either side of it. The clock over the doorway said eight-twenty. People wearing ribbons and boutonnieres were hurrying in and out of the doors. We crossed Broad Street and started edging through the crowd to the entrance. Tony had his Fabulous Fifty identification card in his hand. "Excuse me, Fabulous Fifty," he kept saying. I repeated it after him; people turned to look, and when they saw the card they let us squeeze past them. At the door we found ourselves opposite two men wearing Fabulous Fifty badges. "I can't help it if they're not all here yet," one of them was saying. "We have to take the picture before we leave." I recognized him as the man who had taken our coupons. "Hello," I said.

"Well, hello there, boys! I remember you, the orphans, right? I told you about them, Ralph."

"Sure enough. Come right in, boys," the other man said, and held up the velvet rope. "Mighty plucky work. Congratulations!"

"Thanks," Tony said and ducked under the rope. I hung back on the other side, but Ralph took my arm and pulled me under. "C'mon fellas, don't waste time. We have a lot to do before the train leaves." He put a hand on each of our shoulders and walked us into the lobby and across a red carpet toward the elevators. I was scared. Tony winked at me. "This way, gentlemen." A pretty girl wearing a red, white, and blue sash led us to a decorated table near the elevator doors and another girl pinned a big Fabulous Fifty rosette on Tony. When she started to pin one on me, I drew back. "Ooh, did I stick you?" she said. I blushed, and both girls laughed. Well, so what, I thought. I let her pin the rosette on me, and the first girl led Tony and me into the elevator. What am I doing? I thought. "What the hell," Tony whispered in my ear.

"Congratulations, boys," the elevator operator said. "Thank you," I mumbled automatically. I couldn't believe what was happening and I must have looked it. The girl took my arm. She wore her hair in a blond bob and had a beautiful complexion. She smiled up at me, "Don't be shy, there's lots more to come. We're going to meet Mr. Summerhill, that's the publisher, and then have our picture taken. What's your name?"

"I'm Sol Janus, and this is Tony Ammanati. He's the president of our club, and he's really—"

"Roof! Here we are," the elevator operator said. "Have a great time, boys. You got nice sunshine for the picture."

"Thank you," I said.

"My name's Janet," the girl said. "I work in the copy department. I don't get to go to New York, but I was picked to help out here. It's nice to meet you, Tony and Sol." She shook hands with each of us, and when we went out on the roof she squeezed my hand against her side and kept holding on to it. I wondered how old she was. "Isn't this fun? Aren't you excited?"

"I'll say," Tony said. There was maybe a hundred people standing around in the bright sunshine, all of them wearing Fabulous Fifty badges or rosettes. Off to one side a photographer was standing on a ladder adjusting a big camera on a tall tripod. I began to think it might be fun to be in the picture. It wouldn't hurt anyone, and I could sneak out when we went downstairs. "Come over here," Janet said.

We walked over to a group of older men and more girls. I had never seen so many pretty girls in my life. We were introduced to Mr. Summerhill, to the circulation manager, and to Harry Johnson, the director of the Fabulous Fifty contest. All of them congratulated me. I kept saying, "Thank you very much, sir," hesitantly at first, and then more and more easily. Harry Johnson went out in front of the crowd with a megaphone and called, "Welcome, everybody! Now let's line up, we want to make sure you're all here for the picture." *Uh oh,* I thought. One of the girls handed him a list, and as he read off names people held up their hands and he checked them off. "Hmm, one short," he said. The girls pointed behind him, where an older man wearing a boutonniere was dozing in a wheelchair. A lady hurried up and wheeled the man into the picture line. "Sorry," she said. "That's the whole list," Mr. Johnson said with a big smile. Everyone was there all right; there were so many other people around they never thought to check for an extra. I felt as if I were walking a tightrope.

"My name is Harry Johnson, but I want you all to call me Harry," Mr. Johnson said in a big booming voice. "I'm the contest director, and I'll be going to New York with you. If there's anything you need, don't hesitate to ask me or one of our fine group of assistants. We're here to make sure you have a grand time, and we want you to think of us as part of a big happy family." Then he introduced us to Mr. Summerhill, who congratulated us and made a speech about the *Clarion* encouraging free enterprise and sportsmanlike competition. Tony smiled sideways at me. Mr. Summerhill finished by telling us to enjoy our reward and have fun, and we all cheered and applauded.

The photographer climbed up the ladder and ducked under his black cloth, and the assistants bustled around arranging us into a curved line facing the camera. Harry and Mr. Summerhill stood in the middle of the line, and the girls and assistants knelt in a row in front, holding a big sign that said FABULOUS FIFTY 1921. "Okay, everyone, a big smile, and hold it!" Harry boomed. We grinned, the photographer squeezed his bulb, and the camera pivoted slowly across the line, making a noise like a big windup toy.

"Good!" the photographer called from under his cloth. Tony winked and I winked back. Janet walked over to us again.

"I wish I was going with you," she said to me.

"I do too."

"But I'll be here when you get back." She couldn't be that much older than me, I decided. "Hey, boys! Nice to see you!" It was the fat man who had been in line when we brought in our coupons. He held out his hand. "Sam Hart. Believe me, when I heard your forty-six thousand, I didn't think I had a chance. I just squeaked in—number forty-nine."

"That's great, Mr. Hart. Congratulations."

"Call me Sam, everybody does. I have a real estate office up in Olney. Hey, isn't this something?"

"It sure is," Tony said.

"All right, everybody, the buses are waiting," Harry called. As we moved slowly past him toward the elevators the lady pushing the wheelchair was saying to him,

". . . start out, but I don't know how much he's up to."
Janet stood very close in front of me in the elevator, and I
didn't mind at all. Maybe—maybe nothing, I suddenly
realized when we passed the fourth floor; I had to get out
of here. I figured I could slip aside in the lobby and sneak
down the back stairs that Joe Kolaks had shown us. As the
elevator slowed, I covered the Fabulous Fifty rosette with
my hand and tensed myself to move fast when the doors
opened.

"There they are!" A brilliant flash blinded me, then
another and another. The path from the elevator to the
front door was cordoned off with red velvet ropes, and
press photographers lined the ropes on both sides. "Hey,
Fabulous Fifty!" "Look over this way!" "Smile!" "Are you
having fun?" Every time I looked up another flash went off.
I kept grinning blindly and groped my way to the front
door with Tony. Somewhere I lost Janet in the crush. Okay,
I thought, I'll get away outside.

Not a chance: The velvet ropes led straight down the
steps and across the sidewalk to the door of a bus covered
with red, white, and blue decorations. THE FABULOUS FIFTY
was lettered across the side of the bus. Another set of
photographers lined the ropes, or maybe it was the same
ones running around; I was too dazzled to tell. Behind
them a band was playing, and behind the band was a mob
of people cheering and waving at us. I followed Tony—
there was nothing else to do—and halfway down the steps
he began waving back to people. "You know them?" I
asked.

"No, but what the hell, give them a thrill."

Harry motioned us onto the bus, and I realized that

there were two more buses decorated the same way behind it. "Not bad, eh?" Tony said. Okay, I thought, so I'll ride to the station.

Two motorcycle policemen pulled out ahead of us, then came Mr. Summerhill in a big Cunningham limousine, and two red Kissel roadsters filled with girls waving pennants, and then us. People kept waving at us, and Tony waved back; he was loving every minute of it. This can't go on, I thought, I have to get to school. Halfway to the station a horrible thought struck me: Suppose it was the same there? It couldn't be, I decided, Broad Street Station was too big. There had to be some place where I could slip out. Tony was already trading coupon-collecting stories with Sam Hart, who was sitting across the aisle. "Hey, Tony," I whispered.

"What, sport?"

"You have to help me get out of this at the train station."

He looked at me in surprise. "Whatdya mean? This is great, ain't it? Quit worrying and enjoy yourself. So what if they make a little mistake?"

I looked around nervously. No one was paying attention to us, they were all laughing and talking a mile a minute. When we pulled up at Broad Street, I got a cold feeling in my stomach; there was another aisle of velvet ropes lined with people and photographers leading into the station and across the concourse. First they unloaded the band and the contest officials, and then they opened our door. Lots of policemen wearing white gloves stood around grinning at us. What if I got arrested? I could see it on the front page: YOUTH STOWS AWAY WITH FABULOUS

FIFTY. Tony jumped off the bus and I followed him across another red carpet while the band played and the flashes went off. I walked slowly toward the train like a convict on his way to jail.

Tony was waving to people as if he were the mayor when we boarded the train. Harry Johnson ran back and forth between the two reserved cars carrying a sheaf of papers and mopping his brow. "Everybody here?" Most people were talking and introducing each other, not paying much attention to him. "We have to take a count and make sure nobody got lost on the bus." A few people laughed and I clenched again. Tony got up. "Sit tight," he said. "If they call my name, you answer." He went up to the vestibule at the forward end of the car, and I saw him talking to Sam Hart. Meanwhile Harry Johnson was working his way up from the other Fabulous Fifty car behind us. "Thirty-three," he said as he passed me. I turned to watch him count the remaining seats. "Forty-six, forty-seven, forty-eight, forty-nine." Tony and Sam were nowhere in sight. "I only got forty-nine," Harry called to the assistant at the back of the car. "We have to count again." When he went back to the rear car, Tony slipped into the seat beside me and Sam Hart sat down across the aisle and gave me a big wink. My stomach turned into a small block of ice. "Don't worry, he's okay," Tony whispered.

Harry Johnson was back to me. "Thirty-three," he said again. I sat perfectly still and listened. "Forty-seven, forty-eight, forty-nine, fifty, fifty-one. Fifty-one?"

The assistant coming down the aisle said, "Well, forty-nine and fifty-one averages fifty. At least we know they're all here." The train whistle gave two blasts.

"Right," Harry said, brightening. "That's what's important." The train lurched and began to move. The band on the platform struck up "Give My Regards to Broadway." I looked out the window; Janet was standing there, and I waved to her. She blew me a kiss. "New York, here we come," Tony said.

CHAPTER 24

"Pennsy K-Four Pacific. The best passenger engine in the world," Sam said. It was my first train ride, and I was thrilled by the powerful sounds of our locomotive. It dwarfed the grimy little switch engines on Delaware Avenue. "This is Number three-seven-seven-five, she's practically new," Sam said. "She was built at Altoona last year."

"How do you know?"

"It's my hobby. Know what color she's painted?"

"I thought it was black."

"Nope, that's Brunswick green. Hardly anybody knows that. Tony here says you're a pretty smart fella. I'll take you up to meet the engineer when we get to New York if you want, maybe get a look inside the cab."

"Thanks, I'd like that. I don't feel so smart right now, though."

Sam leaned across the aisle and lowered his voice. "Tony told me all about it. The way I figure it, you got every right to be here. If you guys had divided your coupons in half and sent in twenty-three thousand each, you'd both still be in the top half. And if they take an extra guy on the trip, so what? Summerhill can afford it, that's for sure."

"And guess what?" Tony broke in. "He knows Harry Johnson."

"That's right," Sam said. "He used to have a travel agency in North Philly, and he's a good guy." He reached across and patted my arm. "My advice is to take it easy and enjoy yourself." He hoisted himself out of the seat. "I hear they're gonna have some snacks when we get rolling. I'll go find out."

I sat back and thought about it. "See, I told ya," Tony said.

"I'm still not sure. What about school? What about money?"

"You can go to school anytime. And who needs money? They're gonna take care of everything. I'm tellin' ya, Sam's right. You know why he got on?"

I shook my head.

"He was mad at the paper 'cause he thought they were charging too much for his advertising, and also he was crazy to ride on the special train. He gave his customers a break on real estate commissions in exchange for all their Fabulous Fifty coupons. That's how he got his nine thousand."

Sam came back and sat down. "They're going to serve refreshments after we clear the city." The train started to slow down, and the engine whistle blew a long dash. "*T*," I said.

"*T* what?" Sam asked.

"*T* in Morse code."

He laughed. "That, my boy, is locomotive whistle code for approaching a station. This is North Philly." Suddenly we were sliding through the station; the platforms were jammed with people waving and cheering. "Ain't this great?" Tony said. "Did you see the doll in the blue dress?" The train began to pick up speed again. I could hear the roar of the exhaust and feel the throb of the engine through the seat of my pants; it was thrilling.

"Here we are, folks." One of Harry's assistants put a carton down in the aisle. "We have extra sizes, but you may have to trade around to get fitted." He gave each of us a straw boater with a red, white, and blue band that said Fabulous Fifty. There was a Fabulous Fifty cane, a Fabulous Fifty button, Fabulous Fifty tie clasps and lapel pins and fountain pens. The *Clarion* was making sure that we'd be recognized in New York. "My name is Dan," the assistant said. "And there are plenty of spares, so don't worry if you lose something." He handed each of us a Fabulous Fifty watch fob. "But I don't have a watch," I said.

"Just tuck the end with the clip down in your watch pocket and it'll stay by itself." He showed me how. "Right, that's terrific. Looks just like you had a watch on the other end." By the time he finished outfitting us we looked like the cast of a Fourth of July minstrel show. "Ain't this a killer?" Tony asked, tilting his boater forward like a vaudeville star. Dan's watch had said eleven-thirty, and my school pass was good until eleven o'clock. I wondered what my father would do when he found out I was playing hooky.

"Ah, there they are," Sam said. "I'm famished." Two assistants were pushing a cart up the aisle from the back of the car. They came alongside and offered us chicken salad sandwiches and a grape-colored drink. I was hungry too, I realized as I took a sandwich. "Want some punch?" the assistant asked. "Bug juice," Sam laughed. "Sure, we'll try it. You got an extra sandwich?"

"Coming right up, sir. We're going to have a big lunch at the hotel."

"Good, this'll hold me till then."

The sandwich tasted delicious, but the paper napkin only took about half the mayonnaise off my hands. "Me too," Tony said. "C'mon, let's go wash. I gotta take a leak anyway." There was a line at the lavatory in our car. I followed him back to the rear door. The noise between the cars was terrific, the floor plates clanked and shifted from side to side, and I could glimpse the ties blurring by underneath and smell the engine smoke; I loved it. There was only one man waiting to use the toilet in the rear car. We introduced ourselves; he was a Cadillac salesman from West Philly named Jim Hilferty. "My boss was so excited when I won that he gave me the whole week off with pay. I'm gonna owe my wife a big vacation, though." The lavatory door opened, and he went in. "Well, well," a deep voice said from the nearest seat, "If it ain't little Ammanati."

I didn't recognize the man, but I would have known the voice anywhere: It was Joe Morello. I didn't know whether to run or what. "Hi, Joe," Tony said.

"Hi kid, are you having fun?"

"I am so far."

"Who's this?"

"This is my friend Sol Janus. He's the vice president of our club. See, we shared our coupons."

"Well, everybody has their little schtick, right? Wait a minute; Janus? Oh, yeah," he said, "now I remember." He looked me up and down, and I realized that I was bigger than him. "You kids did all right. Janus, if you need work sometime, come see me."

"Yes, sir, thank you." Like hell I will, I thought. Jim Hilferty came out and Tony went in. "That feels better,"

Jim said. "Trains always make me have to pee. Oops." He looked around. "It's okay, but I should have checked. My seat is right behind those two women." There were two women in the Fabulous Fifty. One was Mrs. Markevich, and the other was a lady named Dora Mendel who had a dress shop in Wynnefield. Jim said she was a widow whose husband had loved baseball, and her customers saved enough coupons to get her on the trip. "She's a nice woman," Jim said, "but that Markevich dame is a real witch."

I had seen Mrs. Markevich on the bus. The *Clarion* picture made her look like a sweet grandma, but up close she looked like a bundle of steel wires. "She smokes these black cigarettes nonstop," Jim said. "I hate to see a woman smoke. There's something cheap about it."

"Right," Morello said. "It's almost as bad as them voting."

"Your turn," Tony said to me. I went into the bathroom and washed my hands and face. I was surprised at how gritty I felt, but flushing the toilet was a bigger surprise. It went right out on the tracks! You could see the roadbed speeding by and feel the cold air rushing in. When I came out, Dan, the contest assistant, was standing with Jim and Joe Morello and Tony; they were all laughing. "That's pretty good," Joe said. "I can't remember jokes worth a damn."

"I write down the punch lines," Jim said. "You need jokes in my business." He turned to Dan. "Who's the old guy in the wheelchair?"

Dan lowered his voice. "That's number fifty, Mr. Leonard. He only sent in eight hundred fifty-three coupons, and the paper gave him what they called 'special credit' for the rest of his eight thousand. I hate to say it about a cripple, but he's really awful."

Back in my seat I listened to the locomotive whistle as we thundered across New Jersey. It blew a long dash for a station maybe a dozen times. "That could be a junction point too," Sam said. Twice it blew *U*: dit-dit-dah. "That's a train meeting point or a passing siding with a waiting train. We get to pass because we're a Class One express." Every once in a while the engineer would blow a *Q*: dah-dah-dit-dah. I could tell that he liked that one, because he really leaned into it and made the whistle howl. It gave me shivers. "That's a grade highway crossing," Sam said. "You wouldn't believe the number of farmers who think they can beat a locomotive to a crossing with a horse and wagon."

Harry Johnson walked up on one of his regular tours and shook hands with Sam. "I finally got a minute to talk. Everything okay, Sam?"

"Hunky-dory, Harry. Have you met the boys here?"

"I sure have. Tell you something, I like having some nice young folks like you along. We have a couple of real lulus in the back car."

"You mean Mrs. Markevich?"

"Well, you wouldn't want to meet her in a dark alley, but we have some others, I can tell already, nothing's going to be good enough for them. They wouldn't be happy if you gave them Mary Pickford on a silver platter. I've run a lot of tours in my time, and I can spot a loser a mile away. I like people to enjoy themselves, you know what I mean?" He grinned and tried to rumple my hair, but I ducked. "Too big for that, eh?"

He walked on up the car. I couldn't tell whether he knew about me and was just letting me ride to New York or what. Just then the train dived into a tunnel under the Hudson River, and when we came up we were on Manhattan Island. New York! All I could see was a concrete wall, but my nose was glued to the window. "Next stop, Pennsylvania Station," Dan called.

"Stick close to me when we get off, Sol," Sam said.

CHAPTER 25

Teeeeeee—I whistled along with the locomotive as the train began to slow down. People were taking their luggage from the overhead racks and piling it in the aisles. The train conductor walked through the car and stopped at our seat. "Have a good ride, boys?"

"It's wonderful," I said. "Is this the fastest train on the line?"

He laughed. "Not by a long shot. You have to ride the Broadway Limited for that. If the White Sox had won the pennant, you'd have been on the Broadway instead of the subway."

"Hey, that's pretty good," Sam said.

"Thank you, sir. You have a good visit."

Blue-uniformed station officials and porters wearing red caps appeared on the platform as the train stopped. I was surprised that there weren't any velvet ropes at this end. "New York is a big town," Sam said. "C'mon with me."

"Everybody stay together!" Harry was calling, but Sam hurried me along the platform to the head of the train. Just as we came up to the locomotive there was a tremendous screeching hiss and a cloud of steam shot out from the front of the engine. I was so scared I jumped a yard in the air. I thought something was broken or that the boiler was going to explode. When I turned around, Sam was laughing. "They're just blowing off the cylinder cocks." The engineer stood at the cab ladder looking at his watch. He wore a blue-striped cap and overalls and heavy gloves with long cuffs. He was smoking a big cigar, and he looked like the boss of everything in sight. "Howdy," Sam said. "That was a great ride. Sure like the way you handle your cutoff."

The engineer nodded gravely. "Thank you, sir. It's nice to talk to someone who knows about it."

"Like to introduce you to my young friend Sol Janus. This was his first train ride, and I was wondering if you might let him have a look in the cab."

The engineer looked at me sternly; I was sure he was going to say no. Then his face broke into a grin. "Sure, young fella, come on up. You too, if you like, sir. Watch yourself. Sol, is it?"

"Yes, sir." I followed him up the ladder. "I'm Abby Wood. This's my fireman, Norm Handy." The fireman waved a glove at us. His face was streaked with soot, and he wore a sweat-soaked red kerchief around his neck. "Show young Sol the fire, Norm." Norm pressed a steel pedal, and the fire doors swung open with a clang. I felt a rush of heat on my face. Inside was what looked like a lake of fiery crystals. It was so hot that everything shimmered; I could only look at it for a few seconds.

"That's what makes us go," Norm said. He slung in a shovelful of coal, pressed another pedal, and the fire doors slammed shut. Everything was bigger, hotter, dirtier, and noisier than I expected. It was wonderful. Wait till I told Tony! Wait till I told Paul and Robert! I leaned out the side of the cab. The tail end of the Fabulous Fifty was disappearing up a flight of stairs, and Dan was walking along the platform with a worried expression.

"We ought to go," I said. "I think they're looking for us."

"Right," Abby said, and pointed to the whistle cord. "Give her a toot before you leave." I couldn't believe it. I grabbed the wooden handle and blew Q: dah-dah-dit-dah. It was deafening inside the station. Abby burst out laughing. "That'll wake 'em up," he said to Norm.

When Dan saw us coming, he broke into a trot. "C'mon, you two, we couldn't get the count right."

"Gee, that's too bad," Sam said, and winked at me.

Despite what he had said, the scene at the curb was like Philadelphia, with even more people watching. The buses had the same Fabulous Fifty signs, and there were photographers with cards from *The New York Times* stuck in their hatbands taking pictures. Tony waved nonstop. Harry gave the *okay* sign to the bus ahead, and as we drove off, the assistants passed out tourist maps of New York. The outside of Pennsylvania Station looked like the Greek temples in our history books, but there were dozens of buildings taller than anything in Philadelphia. The people on the streets seemed in more of a hurry than at home. "What hotel are we staying at?" someone called to Harry.

"Why, the best, of course," he boomed back. "The Plaza."

"Is it nice?" I asked him.

"Is it *nice*?" Harry looked around the bus, playing it for all he could. "Don't you read the *Clarion*, son? That's where the *kings* stay." There was a wave of laughter. "Look out the window, folks, Times Square coming up."

The New York Times was straight ahead on an island in the middle of the street. So that's why they call it Times Square, I thought. The bus turned right on Forty-second

Street, and we could see big signs for Mary Pickford in *Little Lord Fauntleroy,* and Douglas Fairbanks in *The Three Musketeers.* "That's Bryant Park and the Public Library on the right," Sam said. "We'll probably take Sixth Avenue up to the hotel." Sure enough, the bus turned left on Sixth. I watched out the window and followed our route on the map; they could have sold me Pennsylvania Station if they threw in the trains.

The Plaza was right across from Central Park. While I waited for Tony to get off the bus I looked up, trying to count the floors. "Seventeen!" I said. "It must have a thousand rooms."

"C'mon, kid," Joe Morello said, "you're holding up the line." It was no use. When we walked into the lobby I could only stop and stare at the marble columns and the giant ferns and the dressed-up people. After a few minutes Dan came over and told us to meet our bellhops near the elevators. Our bellhop looked at Tony's suitcase and my schoolbag. "You're in room six forty-one. Only these for the two of you?"

"Yeah," Tony said. "We're sharing one."

The bellboy shrugged and we followed him into the elevator. "Six, please," he said smartly to the operator. He was small and slim with slicked-down black hair, and he wore what looked like a band uniform with lots of brass buttons, and a little round cap held on his head by a chin strap. I thought that he couldn't be much older than me. "This way, please." We followed him along a hall, and he set the bags down and unlocked the door of room 641. We followed him in. The room had two beds with nightstands, a big bureau, and two chairs with a low table between them.

There were bedspreads on the beds, pictures on the walls, lamps on the nightstands and the table, and a telephone. Everything looked brand-new, like Paul's house. I must have had my mouth permanently open.

The bellboy set Tony's suitcase on a folding stand, turned on the lights in the room and the bathroom, and showed us how to adjust the radiator. "You can see the park from our windows," I said.

"Yep, it's a nice room. Been to New York before?"

"No, never."

"You guys won that newspaper contest, huh?"

"Yep, we did," Tony said.

"That's all right. I wish I was going to the Series."

"You worked here long?" Tony asked.

"About a year. It's okay. You meet all kinds of people. The job doesn't pay much, but they count on you getting tips."

"Oh, right," Tony said. There was an awkward silence; I didn't have any idea how much to tip. "What's your name?" I asked.

"My real name's John Walter, but everyone calls me Tiny."

"I'm Sol, and this is Tony." We shook hands. "Look, Tiny, we've never done this before, and we don't have a lot of money. How much are we supposed to tip you?"

"Well the rich guys tip two bits a bag. The real rich guys and the drunks sometimes even tip a buck."

"We ain't rich," Tony said. "Sol doesn't even have any extra clothes here."

"Still," I said. I fished in my pocket and found fifteen cents.

"Naw, that's okay," Tiny said.

"No, you keep it."

"Okay. I'll see you around the hotel. Let me know if you need anything. You know what I mean?" He winked at us.

"We will," Tony said, and winked back.

"Oh, here's your keys. Have a good time in New York, fellas," he said, and closed the door.

CHAPTER 26

I wandered around the room looking at everything and then sat down on a bed. How was I going to get out of this? I was too dazed to think clearly. Tony was unpacking his clothes into one side of the bureau. "That Tiny is okay," he said thoughtfully.

"The bellboy?"

"Yep. He's a good guy." He closed his suitcase and put it in the closet. "Might as well get it out of the way for the week."

That reminded me that I was wearing the only clothes I had. "Listen, Tony, I have to get back to Philadelphia."

"Why?"

"Because I'm not supposed to be here. I could get arrested or something."

"Bullshit. You collected coupons, didn't you? Hell, if we divided our coupons by five we'd still have more than Sam."

"But that isn't how they counted it. Besides, I only have these clothes."

"They gotta have a laundry in this place. Look, we'll share my stuff. We'll have enough." Socks and handkerchiefs maybe, I thought. I was thirty pounds heavier than Tony and I could never fit into his shirts and pants. Maybe I could just not get dirty. There was a knock on the door; it was Dan. "Are you guys unpacked? We have a luncheon downstairs and then a sightseeing tour."

"We'll be right down," Tony said and shut the door again. "C'mon, sport, we won the contest and we can handle this. The worst thing they can do is send you home, and I'll give you ten to one they won't. They don't want any bad publicity. You ain't feelin' softhearted about them payin' for you?"

"No, I know they can afford it."

"Right, they got money comin' out of their ears. Let's go to lunch and see what happens. We got nothin' to lose."

I hesitated, and then I thought about Cissie. "Okay, I'll try it."

Lunch was easy. There were plenty of places, and the guy in the wheelchair never showed up. Sam's appetite was amazing. "If he keeps eating like this, he's gonna need two seats on the way home," Tony whispered to me. After lunch two tour buses with guides took us around the city. Even with a map I couldn't keep track of it all. We saw the Metropolitan Museum of Art, the Brooklyn Bridge, Greenwich Village, the Battery—there was something to see everywhere you looked. The tall buildings were the most impressive. "The Woolworth Tower has a total height of seven hundred ninety-two feet and one inch," the guide announced. "It is covered with self-cleaning terra cotta and is the tallest building in New York and the second-tallest structure in the world."

"What's the tallest?" I asked.

"The Eiffel Tower, in Paris, nine hundred eighty-four feet."

In school they had drilled into us that the Philadelphia City Hall was 537 feet high and one of the tallest city halls in the world. The Woolworth Tower looked twice as high, and City Hall sure wasn't self-cleaning.

When we came back to the hotel the lobby was filled with expensively dressed men smoking cigars. Every conversation was about the World Series, and we overheard lots of betting. We were waiting for the elevator when Tiny came by with a couple of suitcases. "Six to five on the Giants is the going rate," he whispered. "They figure there's about two hundred grand on the first game."

Tony whistled. "That's out of our league." We were supposed to get ready for dinner. I sat down on the edge of the bed and realized that I was very tired. "Boy, I could use a nap."

Tony laughed from the bathroom. "A nap! This is the most fun of anything I ever did. Wait till we tell those guys at home."

Home. My drowsiness evaporated and I sat straight up. It had to be about six o'clock. "My folks don't know where I am."

"Call 'em up."

"Long distance? It must be expensive."

"Not for the *Clarion*, it ain't."

I picked up the phone, and a voice said, "Plaza operator, can I help you?"

"Yes, please. I'd like to call Philadelphia. Mrs. Pavlos Janus."

"Do you have the number in Philadelphia, sir?"

"Lombard four two nine three."

"One moment, please."

The telephone clicked and began ringing. When my mother answered the phone she sounded as if she had been crying. "Yes, Mrs. Janus. There's any trouble?"

"Just a moment, please. Go ahead, sir."

"Hello, Momma."

"Sol! You're all right?"

"I'm fine. I'm at the Plaza Hotel, in New York."

"In New York?"

"Yes, Momma, with Tony. With the contest winners."

"What clothes you're wearing?"

"The ones I wore this morning."

"So tomorrow morning?"

"Momma, don't worry about my clothes. Everything's fine." I heard my father asking something. "At school they know you're in New York?"

"No, but it's all right, I'll be excused." Pray to God, I thought.

"Your father says you should come home."

"Tell him I can't, I have to stay with the group. I don't have train fare."

"So how you'll eat?"

"Don't worry, Momma, the newspaper takes care of everything. Look, the World Series starts tomorrow. I'll see you in a few days. We're both fine, and I'll call you again soon, okay?"

"Your father says he'll fix you good when you come home."

"Okay, Momma, I'll talk to you soon."

"So good-bye."

I felt exhausted. Talking to my mother was like shouting across New Jersey. "C'mon," Tony said. "You just got time to wash before we go downstairs."

I hardly remember that evening. We ate in some big Italian place with red-and-white checkered tablecloths and candles stuck in wine bottles on the table. I dozed off in the bus afterward. Tony woke me, we rode upstairs, I fell into bed in my undershorts and slept like a log.

The next morning I woke up feeling great. I took a bath, borrowed a handkerchief and a pair of socks and decided that the rest of my clothes were clean enough to wear. We sat with Sam Hart and Jim Hilferty at breakfast in the hotel restaurant. The menu was a mystery: *Finnan Haddie, Curried Kidneys, Creamed Chipped Beef on Toast.* For breakfast! What were they? I ordered scrambled eggs and sausage and was surprised when they came with parsley sprinkled on them, and hash brown potatoes. Sam had a whole regular steak like people ate for dinner, and two eggs and a grilled tomato besides. "If Mr. Summerhill is kind enough to pay for it, I'm gracious enough to enjoy it." He smiled as he mopped up the juice in his plate with a piece of toast.

"Here's to that," Jim said, and raised his coffee cup. I think that was the first time that I believed that the *Clarion* was really going to pay for everything.

Back at the room I brushed my teeth using a finger and Tony's toothpaste. The morning was open, and the *Clarion* knew who they were rewarding; after the bus tour you could spend your spare time in the burlesque houses for all they cared, and a lot of the men did. Tony and I looked in the windows of the shops in the Plaza's lobby. "What a rook," Tony said. "You think anyone really buys this stuff?"

"You bet they do," said a voice behind us. I jumped; it was Tiny. "I never even heard you," I said.

"One thing you learn in this job is not to be noticed. How are you guys?"

"Okay. We had a swell breakfast."

"Bet on the game yet?"

"No, why?" Tony said.

"I have a friend who works at the Polo Grounds. He says that even though the odds are six to five for the Giants, the Yanks are gonna win today. He's never been wrong yet."

"We still don't have any money to spare," I said.

"Okay, I'm just trying to do you a favor. I'm betting on the Yanks myself." The front bell rang and he trotted over to the desk. "You really think he's betting on the Yanks?" I asked Tony.

"I think probably. Let's take a walk."

We wandered down Fifth Avenue, looking in the shop windows. As we passed a fancy haberdashery, a plump man standing in the doorway smiled and said, "Hi there, fellas. Congratulations."

"Thanks," Tony said.

He glanced at our boaters with the Fabulous Fifty bands. "You look like a couple of sports." We knew we didn't look like sports. Tony glared at him and started to walk away. "Hey, take it easy," the man said. "I didn't mean anything. You must have worked plenty hard to win that contest."

"What if we did?" Tony said.

"Well, I figured if you were smart enough to win you'd like a quality shop like ours." RINE & WHITWORTH was lettered in gold on the window: THE QUIET DISTINCTION OF OUR CLOTHING IS DUE TO A FAITHFUL INTERPRETATION OF THE TASTES OF THE BEST-DRESSED IN NEW YORK. There were two things on display: "Fine English Ulsters—just in time for the World Series and the football games—$75. First-quality British tweed and worsted suits—$60." The salesman blinked behind gold-rimmed glasses. "Why don't you fellas come in and look around?"

"What for?"

"You might see something you like." He held out his hand. "I'm Bob Rine." I shook it reluctantly. "Sol Janus. This is my friend Tony Ammanati."

"Nice to meet you, Sol." He looked at Tony, who wasn't about to shake hands. "Look, just to show you I'm on the level, I'll give each of you a free tie."

"Really free?" I asked.

"Really, no purchase necessary. For the Fabulous Fifty."

Tony looked at me and shrugged, and we went into the store. The salesman called toward the back, "Tom, you have a minute? There's two gentlemen I'd like you to meet." Tom sauntered up to us with a smooth smile. He was dressed like one of the dummies in the window. Rine sent him an eyebrow signal you could have read a block away: *Suckers,* it said.

"Tom Whitworth," the dummy said. "Glad to have you look around." There was an awkward silence and I looked at Rine. "Oh, Tom," he said, "I told Mr. Janus and Mr.—"

"Ammanati," I filled in.

"—right, Mr. Ammanati about our get-acquainted offer of a free tie." He winked at Whitworth.

Whitworth passed a hand across his brilliantined dark hair. "Sure, Bob, glad you did. We're certainly happy to have fifty distinguished guests from Philadelphia visiting us. Right this way, men."

He took a bright green tie from the bottom tray of a display case, draped it over his hand, and held it against Tony's shirt: "A handsome number." Tony pushed his hand away angrily. "Whatdya think I am, a mick from Fitzwater Street? I ain't wearing any Paddy tie."

Whitworth was taken aback. "How about you, Mr. Janus,

do you see one that you like?" He pointed toward the bottom tray. I didn't know anything about ties. My father had three, all the same, that he wore to his lodge meetings. They were blue with tiny white dots; Greek colors. There was a dark one like that in the next case over. "I'd like that one," I said, pointing to it.

Whitworth pursed his lips, and Rine said, "Ah, that isn't part of the—"

"I like that one too," Tony said. "It's like one my uncle Sal wears."

Rine coughed and gave Whitworth a high sign. "All right, men," he said, "that's the one you'll have."

Whitworth gave him a nasty look and pulled out the ties. "Now what else would you like? How about a shirt to match?"

"We only came in because he said he'd give us free ties," I said.

"And you got them," Whitworth said through clenched teeth. "I thought you might want something from our extensive selection."

"Well, we might," Tony said. "We're here for the whole Series."

"Right, they're here for the Series," Rine echoed. "A whole week." Whitworth wrapped the ties and handed them to us without a word. "Thank you very much," I said, and started for the door.

"Say, men," Whitworth called. "You being Fabulous Fifty winners, I wondered if you had any ideas about how the Series is going to go."

"Sure, we got ideas," Tony said. "You got ideas?" His tone worried me.

Whitworth rubbed his hands together. "Maybe we can reach a little sporting agreement," he said.

"Sure," Tony said. "We'll take the Yanks and one run."

"Is that so?" Whitworth said, ice-cold. "Who's gonna give you a run?"

"You are," Tony said. "The smart money is six to five on the Giants, and you know it." Now it was Rine's turn to look worried. "Well, now," he wheedled. Whitworth flashed him a message: *We have to get them on the hook somehow.*

"Okay, we'll give you a little bet," Whitworth said. "How about twenty bucks?"

"Shake," Tony said, and before I could stop him he did.

CHAPTER 27

"Are you crazy?" I asked Tony angrily when we were back out on the street. "Are you nuts? We can't afford to bet any twenty bucks. How will we pay them if we lose?"

"Relax, greaseball. They took the bet because they think we're a couple of rubes. Don't worry, we ain't gonna lose, I can feel it in my bones. The Yanks got Mays, they got Hoyt, they got Ruth. You heard what Tiny said. Besides, if we lose we just won't show up."

The whole thing gave me the willies. We went up to the room and I unwrapped my new tie for some comfort. Whitworth didn't even take off the price tag. Pure Silk— $2, the tag read. "You got good taste, sport," Tony said. If you remember those ears of corn, two for a penny, you can imagine what a two-dollar tie meant to us. I carefully rewrapped my tie and laid it in my empty bureau drawer.

At lunch Harry Johnson gave out red, white, and blue books of Fabulous Fifty World Series Tickets. He explained that we should keep them with us for identification, but they were just souvenirs; a special section of box seats was roped off for us, and we would be ushered into it as a group every day. Our buses left the hotel at one o'clock, and on the way I read a handout about the Polo Grounds. "It holds thirty-seven thousand people!" I told Tony.

"Yeah, I heard there were people sleeping outside the

park all night to get good places in the ticket line today."

Waiting in line was one thing the Fabulous Fifty didn't have to do. Our buses stopped at the corner of One Hundred and Fifty-fifth Street and Eighth Avenue, and there was a squad of special ushers to take us to our seats. I tried to stay in the middle of the group. "Not bad, eh?" Sam Hart said. "Only twelve hundred box seats in the place, and we must have sixty of them." They were great seats; the boxes reserved for big shots were right below us. I recognized Ban Johnson, the president of the American League, from his picture in the paper. He was a big man with a bulldog scowl around his cigar, and he wore a black bowler hat and a coat with a velvet collar. Judge Landis, the new baseball commissioner, looked over at our group with friendly curiosity. I felt myself flushing when he glanced at me; I couldn't look him in the eye. "There are some people from our hotel." I pointed out a couple in one of the boxes to Tony and Sam. "The lady with the purple hat. I saw her in the lobby after lunch."

"That," Sam announced, "is Mrs. William G. McAdoo, the daughter of President Wilson. The man with her used to be secretary of the treasury."

"No kidding?"

"No kidding." Sam looked through his seating map. "See that family over there, that must be, let's see, box fifty-one? That's Nathan Miller, the governor of New York State. And in front of the McAdoos, that's John Hylan, the mayor of New York. He's going to throw out the first ball."

"Gosh." I never expected to see so many famous people at a baseball game.

"Look over there." Jim Hilferty pointed to a crowd of reporters taking pictures of three men entering the boxes. "That's Irving Berlin, and the guy next to him looks like George M. Cohan."

"The third one is Flo Ziegfeld," Sam put in. "How'd you like to have his job, playing around with those showgirls every day?" He elbowed me in the ribs. "That would be some fun, eh, kid?"

The photographers ran around in a frantic clump from one celebrity to the next. "Can I borrow those for a minute?" Jim asked a man behind him with a pair of field glasses. He looked through them at a box and said, "Now there's a real lady. And I bet those are real sables too." He handed me the glasses and told me where to look. It was a handsome dark-haired woman standing up in a front box. She was wearing a black-and-white dress with furs around her shoulders, and she was smiling and waving at the reporters. "Who is it?" I asked.

"Mrs. Babe Ruth, that's who." I looked again and gave the glasses back. "I never thought it would be this exciting," I said to Tony.

"This is just the beginning, sport."

"There's Colonel Ruppert," Sam said. "He owns the Yankees." Colonel Ruppert was chubby and dapper, with a little mustache and a bow tie. He looked like a southern planter. The idea of somebody owning the Yankees did seem a little like slavery to me.

Suddenly it was two o'clock and the band was playing "My Country 'Tis of Thee." Mayor Hylan threw the first ball out to Phil Douglas, the Giants' starting pitcher, and everyone cheered. I was so excited I hardly noticed the cold breeze. The first batter was Elmer Miller, the Yankee center fielder, and he drove a long single straight to center field. "See," Tony said. "I told you. The Yanks are hitting three hundred and the Giants are only hitting two ninety-eight." I was impressed until I found out that the statistics were printed in the program. That little difference couldn't mean much, I thought. The next batter sacrificed Miller to second base, and then the whole stadium fell silent. As Babe Ruth walked to the box a tremendous roar broke over the field like a wave—the crowd must have cheered for half a minute. Ruth just stood at the plate and waited for the pitch. When it came he walloped a single to center field, and Miller scored. "Wow! Whatdya think of that, sport, one–nothin' in the first inning?" Tony was jumping up and down in his seat. "Boy," Sam said. "I didn't know you were such a Yankee fan."

I envied Tony his ability to let go. Every time I remembered the bet I clenched inside. I was counting on Ruth to keep hitting, but when he came up again in the fourth inning, Douglas walked him. "Before the Series they were saying he might not play because he had an infection in his elbow," Sam said. The man to count on was Carl Mays, the Yankee pitcher, who kept pitching underhanded submarine balls at the Giants' knees. The only man who could hit him was Frankie Frisch, and he was left on base every time.

Neither side scored again until the fifth inning. By that time I had eaten three hot dogs and I was bouncing around in my seat like Tony. The first batter was the Yankee third baseman Mike McNally, who slammed a double to left field. The catcher, Wally Schang, sacrificed McNally to third and I sat forward with expectation. "Damn," Tony said, "it's Mays. He couldn't hit a barn door." Tony was right. Mays struck out, but just as my hopes waned, McNally slid across home plate to the amazement of everyone, especially Frank Snyder, the Giants catcher. "He stole home!" Tony screamed. "He stole home!" The Polo Grounds went wild and I cheered frantically. Two–nothing!

Mays made up for his strikeout by retiring the Giants one-two-three, and the Yanks were batting again. Roger Peckinpaugh, the Yankee captain, was first up. He beat out a slow roller to the shortstop, and then went to second base on a passed ball. The next batter was Babe Ruth. I stood up with half the stadium and watched in disbelief as he struck out. "Nuts," I said. Sam handed me a box of popcorn. "Try that." I just had it open when Bob Meusel slammed a drive to deep left field. "It's a homer!" Tony shouted. Almost: Peckinpaugh scored, but Meusel stopped at third base. His older brother Irish Meusel was the Giants' left fielder, and he made a tremendous throw to George Kelly, the first baseman.

"Why did he do that?" I asked Sam. "Why didn't he cut him off at third?"

"Beats me, he must've seen something." It was another surprise: The run counted, but Bob Meusel was called out for failing to touch first base. Still, we were ahead three to nothing! My stomach was churning with nervousness. Neither side scored in the next two innings, and in the ninth the Giants put Jesse Barnes in as pitcher. For a while it looked like the Yankees were going to score again, but Barnes finally struck out Wally Schang with two men left on base. When Frankie Frisch led off for the Giants he hit another single. I held on to my seat until the next man forced him out at second. George Kelly, the third batter, hit into a double play and the game was over: Yankees 3, Giants 0! Tony stood on his seat cheering and slapped me on the back. "How about that, sport!"

"You were right." I had new respect for Tony's gambling instincts, and the realization that we had actually won began to sink in on the bus ride back to the Plaza. We headed straight for Rine & Whitworth. Rine wasn't around. "Hear the game score?" Tony asked Whitworth.

"Why, no," Whitworth lied. "Giants take it?"

"The Yankees, three to nothing," I said.

"Oh," he said.

"So where's our twenty bucks?" Tony asked.

Whitworth opened the cash drawer. "Well," he said, as if he just found out, "Bob took our receipts to the bank, and I don't want to open up short of cash tomorrow." He took out a ten-dollar bill. "How about this on account?"

"Okay," Tony said.

"With an IOU," I said.

"Right, with an IOU," Tony repeated. "We know you guys are good for it."

Whitworth wrote out an IOU for ten dollars and gave it to me. "You boys care to make a bet on tomorrow's game? Say another twenty?"

"Sure," Tony smiled. "Who do you want?"

"Well, you had the Yanks today," Whitworth oiled, like fair is fair.

"And the bookies say they're a sure thing tomorrow, right? Okay, we'll take the Giants."

"You'll take the Giants?" Whitworth tried to hide his smile.

"And five runs."

"Five runs! You're out of your mind, kid."

"C'mon," Tony said. "The Yanks wiped them today and they weren't even trying. Ruth's just gettin' warmed up. You know they're gonna win tomorrow."

"But I'm not giving any five runs."

Tony looked serious. I was filled with admiration for his talent. "Well," he said slowly, "the odds are on the Yanks eight to five. We gotta have some chance. Well, okay, four runs then."

"That's a tough bet," Whitworth pleaded.

"That's it," Tony said, turning away.

"Okay," Whitworth said weakly, and we shook hands. Here we go again, I thought. As we started to leave I noticed a display of shirts. "Do you have any shirts my size?" I asked Whitworth.

"Loosen your tie and I'll measure you. Fifteen neck and, let's see, a thirty-two sleeve. "Say—" he indicated the IOU still in my hand. "Would you like to take that out in trade?"

"That ain't fair, you get the stuff wholesale," Tony said.

"I'll split the difference with you," Whitworth said. "Twenty percent off, how's that?"

"I'll take it," I said. I left the store with three shirts, three pairs of socks, three handkerchiefs, and three sets of underwear. "You're nuts to take that stuff instead of dough," Tony said when we were back in the room. He sat in a chair fingering his ten-dollar bill while I filled up my bureau drawer. I felt cleaner already.

CHAPTER 28

Thursday morning we saw Tiny in the lobby and told him about our winning bet on the Yankees. "Stay with 'em today," he counseled. "The odds were eight to five last night, and I heard a bookie asking four to one this morning. I don't think he had any takers, though." Four to one sounded pretty steep to me; I wondered whether four runs would be enough. I glanced at Tony and he winked. What the heck, I thought, we did okay yesterday. I was amazed to find myself thinking like a sport; I had never been one even though Tony called me that a lot. The clothes were part of it. I boarded the Fabulous Fifty bus feeling like a new man in clean Rine & Whitworth underwear, shirt, and socks. When we arrived at the park I wished I had a sweater too, because it was even chillier than Wednesday.

The starting pitchers for the second game were Art Nehf for the Giants and Waite Hoyt for the Yankees. In the program Hoyt was called "The Brooklyn Schoolboy." "Gosh, he's only nineteen," Tony read. "They signed him at sixteen. How about that! John McGraw comes up to you on the corner lot and says, 'Want to pitch for the Yankees?' "

"McGraw may have spotted him, but Huggins has him now," Sam said. "And he's a hell of a pitcher, nineteen or not."

Hoyt didn't waste any time proving it. Governor Miller threw out the first ball, and Hoyt struck out George Burns and retired the Giants one-two-three. The third man out was Frankie Frisch. "Gosh, Hoyt is really hot, isn't he?" I said to Tony.

"Yes, darn it," he muttered.

Art Nehf was pretty hot too. He threw left-handed, and the first two innings were pitching duels without any score. Then in the third inning the Yankees started a rally with two outs. Hoyt singled, and Nehf walked Roger Peckinpaugh and Babe Ruth. Bases loaded! I was scared silly. We stood up in anticipation, Nehf put on the pressure, and Bob Meusel popped a fly ball to shortstop to end the inning. Hoyt froze the Giants again one-two-three, and the Yanks loaded the bases again with two outs. Even Tony looked nervous. This time Hoyt grounded to second, and Aaron Ward scored the first run. Yankees 1, Giants 0. We were still three runs to the good.

Tony and I were keeping quiet. At the beginning of the eighth inning the score was still 1 to 0, and I felt as if I had been holding my breath for the whole game. Hoyt was still knocking the Giants down as fast as they came up, but in the bottom of the eighth the Yanks finally solved Nehf's pitches. Peckinpaugh singled, but was forced out at second base when Ruth singled behind him. Then Bob Meusel came to bat. As Nehf was winding up for the first pitch, Meusel stepped out of the batter's box and glared at Earl Smith, the Giants' catcher. "Did you hear what he called me?" Meusel asked the umpire. The ump nodded, cautioned Smith, and waved Meusel back into the box. "Play ball," he ordered. Meusel swung at Nehf's first good pitch and hit a long single to center field. Ruth, moving deceptively fast, scored on the throw-in, and Meusel went to second. "We're okay," Tony murmured to me. "We still have two runs." The next man up was Wally Pipp, the Yankee first baseman. He grounded to second and Meusel made it to third base. "Man, he's fast," Tony said.

Meusel took a long, cocky lead off third and danced around, taunting the Giants catcher. "Look out, Smith," he called. "I'm gonna steal it right under your nose." Smith picked up his mask for a second and swore at Meusel; we could see it clearly from our box. Second baseman Aaron Ward was up next. Nehf pitched to him, Smith threw the ball back, and suddenly Meusel was sliding toward home plate while the crowd roared. Smith was so rattled that he dropped the throw from Nehf; the umpire spread his arms, palms down: "Safe!" Smith threw his mask on the ground and fired a burst of profanity at Meusel and the ump. "He stole home!" Tony shouted. "Did you see that, he stole home!"

Sam looked at him in astonishment. "Hey, I thought you were rooting for the Yankees."

"That was yesterday," Tony said sullenly. We stood up as Nehf pitched to Ward again. "C'mon, there's two outs, fan him," Tony muttered. Please, no more runs, I prayed. Nehf threw, Ward fouled a high ball over toward first base and George Kelly put it away. "Yayyy!!" we cheered in unison, and clapped each other on the back. Jim and Sam looked at each other and shrugged; nutty kids, their expressions said. The last half inning was almost a duplicate of the first game. Frisch singled with one out, and George Kelly hit into a double play and ended the game the same way he had the day before.

Tony bounced up and down in the bus all the way to the

Plaza. "Another twenty bucks!" he said to me as we trotted down Fifth Avenue. Rine and Whitworth were both waiting for us this time. "Pretty sharp betting, fellas," Whitworth said.

"We were just lucky," Tony said. "We don't have your experience. How about tomorrow?"

"We have to talk about it," Rine said. He and Whitworth went into the back room. I wandered around the store, looking at luggage and clothes. I had never cared much about clothes, but suddenly I saw a suit that I wanted to own. It was dark blue, with long pants and a vest. The fabric was soft and smooth looking—it would never itch. The price tag said fifty dollars. Well, maybe someday.

Rine and Whitworth came back smiling. "We have a bet," Whitworth said. "Take it or leave it."

"Shoot," Tony said.

"We'll give you the Giants and one run, but no more." Whitworth was rubbing his hands; he could hardly wait to see if we would take it, and I knew why. The papers all said that no team had ever won a World Series after losing two games. Many sportswriters expected the Yankees to make a clean sweep, and obviously Rine and Whitworth did too. Tony didn't. "How much?" he asked.

"Fifty bucks." I guessed that they wanted to cover their losses.

"Okay," Tony said. "If you pay today's bet in cash."

"Here it is," Whitworth said, and handed each of us a ten-dollar bill.

I looked over at the blue suit. "Let's make it a hundred," I heard myself say.

Tony raised his eyebrows. "A hundred?"

"Why not?" Half of that would get me the suit. He looked at me admiringly and shrugged. "Okay with me, sport. What about you guys?"

Rine looked at Whitworth and nodded. We all shook hands. They were smiling when we left.

"Boy, what got into you?" Tony asked me outside. I told him about the suit. He poked me in the ribs. "That's the stuff, pal."

Judge Landis was on the front page of Friday morning's *New York Times*. He fined Earl Smith $200 for using profane language to umpire George Moriarty and Bob Meusel. There was a quote underneath his stern photograph: "I will not tolerate rowdyism of any description on the playing field, and violators will be promptly dealt with."

The third game drew a capacity crowd, but it got off to a bad start for us. We had just sat down when Jim Hilferty pointed to the left field bleachers. "What's going on over there?" He borrowed his neighbor's field glasses again. "It looks like some school kids—yep, they must've snuck into the park." He handed me the glasses, and I watched as a police squad herded them together and wrote down their names. *School kids.* I sat frozen as the cops fanned out to look for other truants. Jim and Sam laughed. "Poor kids, they oughta let them stay," Jim said. "I bet they'd like to be up here with you guys."

"Right, I bet they would, ha ha." My chest felt full of ice cubes until the cops detoured around the wire screen at the end of the box seats. I guess they didn't expect any truants in the boxes.

My relief didn't last long. The starting pitchers that day were Fred Toney for the Giants and Bob Shawkey for the

Yankees, and the first inning was a duel between them with Frankie Frisch's single the only hit for either team. The tempo picked up in the second inning: Bob Meusel doubled for the Yanks, and his brother Irish and Frank Snyder both singled for the Giants. We jumped to our feet when Aaron Ward, the Yankee second baseman, made a spectacular leaping catch of Johnny Rawlings's line drive, and then double-played Irish Meusel at first. More hits, but no score.

The Giants pitching fell apart in the third inning, and after the Yankees batted I was sure we were sunk. First Toney walked Wally Schang. Then Bob Shawkey—the pitcher!—singled to right field. Elmer Miller singled behind him and Schang scored. Tony and I looked at each other: There goes our one run. Toney, under pressure, walked Roger Peckinpaugh, loading the bases. No outs, and guess who was up next? Babe Ruth, that's who. All I could think of was our bet. A hundred bucks! I must have been out of my mind—I had never even seen a hundred bucks.

Ruth didn't strike out this time; he hit a long, slick single to center field and drove in Shawkey and Miller. McGraw gave up on Toney and sent Jesse Barnes in to pitch. Barnes was barely on the mound before Ruth tried to steal second, but he was thrown out. Barnes was nervous too, and he walked Bob Meusel. Then Wally Pipp, the Yankee first baseman, hit a grounder to second and Peckinpaugh scored. Finally Barnes struck out Aaron Ward and it ended. Four nothing, Yankees, and the Giants still hadn't scored a single run in the Series. The papers were right, and we were in trouble.

We could see John McGraw lecturing his team in the

dugout as they waited for their turn at bat. The relief pitcher, Jesse Barnes, came up first and surprised us with a single to left field. George Burns, the center fielder, flied out, but then Dave Bancroft singled to right, and Shawkey walked Frisch. One out and bases loaded; now the pressure was on the Yankees. The Giants right fielder Ross Youngs came up and the whole stadium watched without a sound as Shawkey crumbled, walking Youngs and forcing Barnes home. Then he walked George Kelly and Bancroft scored. That was it for Shawkey. Huggins sent in old Jack Quinn to save the situation, but he was too late; Irish Meusel scored Frankie Frisch, and Johnny Rawlings drove in Youngs. It was tied up, four to four! My scorecard was crushed into a sweat-soaked wad. "What an inning," Sam said. "I need something to eat."

He finished two hot dogs and a sweet roll while both pitchers held the game scoreless for three more innings. Jesse Barnes seemed to have things under control for the Giants. He retired the first three Yankee batters in the seventh inning in order, striking out Elmer Miller on the way. If only we can hold them for two more turns at bat, I prayed.

Dependable Frankie Frisch led off for the Giants in the seventh and singled to center field. We were so used to him being left on base that it was a surprise when Ross Youngs doubled to deep right and George Kelly walked, loading the bases. Tony looked at me and held up crossed fingers. Sure enough, Irish Meusel slammed a double to right field. Frisch and Youngs scored, Kelly went to second base, and Jack Quinn, the Yankees' second pitcher, went to the showers. Rip Collins came in for him and promptly gave up a single to Johnny Rawlings that scored Kelly and Meusel. "Eight to four!" Tony shouted, slapping me on the back.

"Take it easy, it isn't over yet."

Rawlings got too cocky and was caught trying to steal second. I guessed that was the end of the rally, but Frank Snyder, the catcher, singled, and then so did Jesse Barnes and George Burns. The bases were loaded again, with only one out. "This is unbelievable," Jim Hilferty said. Someone had given him a cigar, and it was nearly chewed in half. The next batter was Dave Bancroft, the shortstop and captain of the Giants. He hit a sacrifice fly to left field and Snyder scored after the catch. "Five runs so far this inning!" Sam marveled.

I could tell that Rip Collins was nervous that the Giants had batted around the order and Frankie Frisch was up again. He wilted and walked Frisch. The bases were loaded again for the third time in one inning! "This is unbelievable," Jim said again. Ross Youngs swung a couple of bats and then walked quietly to the plate. Collins gave him a pitch that should have been delivered on a silver platter and Youngs belted it as far into center field as it could go without being a home run. Barnes, Burns, and Frisch all scored on Youngs's triple, and Collins was on his way to the Yankee dugout as soon as Youngs tagged third base. Huggins sent in a fourth pitcher, Tom Rogers, and it was almost a relief when George Kelly hit a slow grounder to him for the third out.

"I believe you boys have just witnessed a record," Sam said. "Eight runs have never been scored in a World Series inning before, as far as I know." I didn't care about the statistics; I just didn't want the Yanks to catch up. They did get another run in the eighth, but the Giants matched it, and Barnes put the Yankee batters away without a slip in the ninth. The final score read Giants 13, Yankees 5. Tony must have lost weight jumping up and down. "The Giants and one run!" he shouted.

When we came back to the hotel I was wrung out. I told Tony I wanted to wash up before we went to collect our bet. There was a crowd around a big box in the lobby, and we walked over to see what it was: WESTINGHOUSE RADIO STATION WJZ PRESENTS THE FIRST WORLD SERIES BROADCAST IN HISTORY. It was an Atwater Kent radio tended by an engineer, and the sign told how a play-by-play description was telephoned from the Polo Grounds to the Westinghouse Electric building in Newark, New Jersey, and rebroadcast by WJZ announcer Tommy Cowan. When we arrived Cowan was giving a review of the game. There was also a big poster showing how radio worked, with pictures and diagrams of the equipment. An elderly man standing nearby shook his head. "It's too much for me. What'll they think of next?"

I went up to our room feeling superior and nervous.

CHAPTER 29

Tony dangled his leg over the arm of a chair. "Well, whatdya say? Shall we go down and collect?"

I ran a comb through my hair one more time. "I guess so." I really didn't believe that Rine and Whitworth would pay off. It was too much money.

They looked the way I expected them to when we walked in: grim. "Hi, fellas," Tony said. Neither of them answered for a while. Then Whitworth said, "What do you guys want?"

I knew right away that what I had worried about was coming true, but Tony looked surprised. "They aren't going to pay us," I blurted.

Rine and Whitworth didn't contradict me, but Tony looked shocked. "What a rotten thing to say! You think these guys are crooks or something?"

I looked back at him blankly.

"This is a classy outfit, you know they're honest. And even if they weren't, I mean, suppose they didn't pay and we told the *Clarion* people? Two young kids like us, we come to New York with the Fabulous Fifty and two guys who run a Fifth Avenue store talk us into betting on the ball games—us, a couple of rube kids—and then they don't pay up when they lose." Tony shook his head as if he couldn't get over how mean I was. "A story like that would be all over the papers in a day. I bet it would cost a store like this a lot of business, besides getting in trouble with the law. But what's the use of talking about something that ain't going to happen? These guys are gentlemen, it says so right in the window."

"Excuse me," I said. "I'm sorry for what I said." Rine looked pale. They looked at each other, then back at us. "We're a little short of cash," Whitworth said.

"How short?" Tony asked.

"We can give you fifty bucks now."

"And another IOU," I said.

Whitworth gave me a look of pure hatred. "Right, and another IOU."

"Well," Tony said after we had collected, "How about—?"

"No more bets," Whitworth said viciously.

"Okay, you don't have to be a sorehead about it." I wanted to check that they still had the blue suit, but this didn't seem like a good time to ask about it.

When we woke up the next morning rain was beating against the windows. "There ain't gonna be any game today," Tony said. At breakfast we all agreed, and the weatherman made it official later; the fourth game was postponed because of rain. We read the papers in our room with Sam Hart. Most of the sportswriters gave the credit for the Giants' eight-run inning to the new rabbit ball. The *Times* ran a piece on the kids that crashed the Polo Grounds. All but one were caught by the stadium police, and the one that climbed back out was nabbed by a truant officer outside. Boy, I thought, they must have tough truant officers in New York. DENIES TRUANCY, the headline said. When they asked the kid why he wasn't in school, he said his grandmother died last week.

"What are you boys going to do this afternoon?" Sam asked.

"Beats me," Tony said. He looked over my shoulder as I turned to the theater pages. "Hey look, the Ziegfeld Follies. I bet that's hot stuff."

"They aren't going to let you into that for a few years," Sam said.

I read through the show titles: *"Blossom Time—"*

"A dog," Sam said. "Too sentimental. I saw the opening in Philly."

"Pot Luck? The Blue Lagoon? The Circle, The Green Goddess, Six Cylinder Love—Who's Ernest Truex?"

"An actor. You kids don't want to see any of that stuff."

"It says here that the *Music Box Revue* has the world's prettiest chorus. I wouldn't mind seeing that."

"They all say that, it's just a lot of blarney."

Suddenly near the bottom of the page I found something I did want to see. "Hey, how about *The Three Musketeers?* It has Douglas Fairbanks."

"That's for me," Tony said and jumped on the bed. "Sheeu, sheeu!" he swished, dueling, and then he jumped off the bed and stuck his outstretched index finger in Sam's stomach. "Take that!"

"You got me," Sam said and sank back in his chair. Tony wiped off his rapier and slid it back into the scabbard. "What time does it start?"

"It says there are two shows, two-thirty and eight-thirty."

"Let's try the two-thirty," Sam said. "Where is the movie playing?"

"At the Lyric. West Forty-Second Street, it says."

"We can take a cab over there."

I realized later how nice Sam was being to us. Most of the men in the group spent their time playing cards or going to burlesque shows. He did seem to enjoy the movie, though. The Lyric was a real movie palace with colored lights and an organ and plush reserved seats. "You really think he does that stuff himself?" Tony asked after Douglas Fairbanks jumped off a wall, swung across a room on a chandelier, and landed fighting two men with his sword.

"All himself," Sam said. "He's a great athlete and swordsman."

"Sshh," someone behind us said.

"I always thought movie stars were sissies," Tony whispered.

"Sshhh!"

I loved the sword fights, and when the movie ended I felt like fencing myself. Tony and I dueled our way around the foyer while Sam went to the men's room. We were waiting near the front door when a smooth-looking man, a not-so-handsome Whitworth, walked up to us. He eyed our Fabulous Fifty buttons. "Enjoying the World Series, boys?"

"We sure are."

"Tomorrow should be a really exciting game with the Giants turning it around like that."

"Probably," I said, while Tony looked the guy over.

"There's a terrific demand for tickets to tomorrow's game," the man said meaningfully, and Tony brightened up. "How terrific?" he asked.

"Ten bucks terrific," the hustler said.

"We have box seats. They're going for twenty on the street," Tony said. How did he know that?

"Twelve-fifty," the man said. "I'm gonna use 'em myself."

"Fifteen bucks," Tony said.

The man shook his head and reached for his wallet. "Jeez, kid, you drive a hard bargain."

Tony took out his book of Fabulous Fifty tickets. "Gimme your book, Sol."

"But those are just—" I began.

"The best seats in the house, mister," Tony finished. A minute later we had our books back, each with one ticket missing and three five-dollar bills in its place. "What a town," I said.

When we got back to the hotel I sat down at a desk in the lobby and wrote a postcard with a picture of the Plaza on the front. I tried to sound grown-up:

Dear Mom and Dad:

I am fine and hope you are too. We had good weather for the first three games, but today it's raining. We're having a wonderful time. Please call Dr. Farnsworth at Central High and tell him where I am. Thank you. Don't worry about anything. Love, Sol.

I had to write very small to fit it all on the card. On the way to buy a stamp I saw Tiny. "Hey, Sol, I'll mail it for you." He lowered his voice. "Tony said you've been doing great on the games. You want me to get you some you-know-what? I know some real cute ones."

"Thanks, Tiny, I better not. How are you doing on the Series?"

"Almost as good as you, but I have to bet with smarter

guys. I'm going to work on those clothes salesmen after you leave."

We both turned at the sound of raised voices by the lobby desk. It was Mr. Leonard, the man in the wheelchair, and Harry Johnson. ". . . They're a lot of crooks," I heard Mr. Leonard saying angrily. I walked over closer and stood behind some palms. "We're doing all we can," Harry said. "It's not easy getting your wheelchair everywhere. We did arrange the special meals and the connecting room for your nurse."

"Not a considerate person in the whole bunch," Mr. Leonard retorted. "No one to carry on a decent conversation with, just a bunch of cheats. Never had a worse time in my life. I never liked baseball anyway."

"What can we do for you?" Harry asked.

"You can send me home, that's what, and pay for it. And don't think I won't tell people what a bunch of lowlifes and cheapskates you are."

Harry threw up his hands. "When would you like to go?"

"Right now, on the next train. Soon as we can."

"I'll see what I can do."

I could hardly wait to get upstairs and tell Tony.

The postcard eased my conscience, and I left for the Polo Grounds on Sunday feeling great. The sun was shining as we climbed the steps to the Fabulous Fifty boxes. When we reached the roped-off section I noticed two men sitting in the middle of it. Dan walked over to them and explained that these were special boxes reserved for the Fabulous Fifty. The men ignored him. He came back and talked to Harry Johnson. Harry went over and asked them to leave. This time one of them reached into his shirt pocket and held up two Fabulous Fifty tickets. "Don't bother me, buddy," he sneered, and the truth suddenly dawned on me.

Harry scowled when he saw the tickets and started to lecture the men; one of them shook his fist at Harry. Neither one was the man we saw at the theater, but Tony looked at me and we edged toward the middle of the group. Harry went away and came back with a head usher. Both men shook their fists at Harry and the usher. The usher went away and came back with two big Irish cops, who grabbed the two men by the backs of their collars and marched them out of the Fabulous Fifty section. I burrowed into the crowd with my back to them. "But dammit, we paid twenty bucks apiece for these seats," one of them complained as the cops hustled him past. We filed into our seats. "Serves them right," Mrs. Mendel said. "They must be crooks." I looked at Tony and he shrugged. I knew I wouldn't do that again.

The big question on Sunday was whether Babe Ruth would play. According to the papers his arm still wasn't healed. At about one-thirty he surprised people on both sides by lumbering out to his usual position in left field. Douglas and Mays were the pitchers, the same two that opened the Series. They were both throwing well, and there were no runs scored in the first four innings. When the Yankees came to bat in the fifth, Wally Pipp, the first baseman, hit a single and was sacrificed to second by Aaron Ward. Then Mike McNally made it to first on a dribbly grounder, but Pipp was tagged out on his way to third. Wally Schang came up next and hit a solid triple that scored McNally. The Yanks stayed ahead by that one run for the next two innings. "Not much excitement today," Tony said when we stood up for the seventh-inning stretch, and I agreed with him.

I guess we should have realized that the Giants were late bloomers after their record seventh inning on Friday. Irish Meusel started the top of the eighth with a triple and then tied the game up on a single by Johnny Rawlings. Then Frank Snyder beat out a bunt, and George Burns lobbed a short double just over Roger Peckinpaugh's head to score them both and put the Giants ahead 3 to 1. Wally Schang came back with a single for the Yankees, but he was forced at second base, and Phil Douglas struck out two more Yankee batters to finish the inning.

"I bet the Giants are gonna come back and win the whole thing," Tony said.

"That's not very likely," Sam said. "Statistically, I mean."

"Even my wife would love it if the Giants won," Jim Hilferty said.

"No team has ever lost the first two games and won the World Series," Sam said. "You can't ignore history."

Tony shrugged. "There has to be a first time." Sam gave him this look like a teacher patting him on the head: *We've seen a few more things than you, my boy.* "Well, I still think they'll win," Tony muttered stubbornly.

The Giants looked like they thought the same thing and started a rally in the ninth that scored another run. That made their lead 4 to 1, but the Yanks still had a chance, because the top of their lineup was at bat. Roger Peckinpaugh grounded out to second base, and then Babe Ruth came up. So far he had grounded out, singled, and struck out. He stood near the batter's box kneading his left arm above the elbow, and he kept his forearm out in front of him with his fingers hooked in his belt until the first pitch. Then he gave us a lesson in how heroes are different from other people by slamming a tremendous home run into the right field bleachers. The Yankee fans stood up and cheered, and so did I. When I sat down Tony looked at me as if I was a traitor; his allegiance was to the team he bet on last. Phil Douglas took care of the next two Yankee batters and it was all over: Giants 4, Yankees 2, and the Series tied up with two games apiece.

CHAPTER 30

We stopped by Rine & Whitworth first thing Monday morning. Rine was there alone, straightening up the cases. His gold-rimmed glasses and round face made him look like a professor. He was humming to himself when we came in. "Oh, good morning, boys."

"How's your cash?" Tony asked.

"Well, to tell the truth, we're still short. In fact, Tom is at the bank now. We have to build up our inventory for the Christmas season."

"Did he tell you that I took some of my winnings in trade last week?" I asked.

"Yes, he did."

"And that he gave me twenty percent off?"

"Yes, he told me." The light dawned in his eyes. "Would you like to take some more in trade?"

"I might." Tony looked disgusted with me.

"That would be fine with us. Is there anything in particular you'd like?"

I walked straight over to the blue suit. "Do you have this in my size?"

"I'll measure you." He was very deft and quick with his tape; you could see that he enjoyed measuring people. "A perfect thirty-four. That should be easy." He went into the back room and was back quickly with a suit. "Here it is." I went into the fitting room and took off my pants. In a moment Rine's arm appeared with the suit pants hanging over it, their bottoms turned up. I put them on and came out and Rine had me stand on a carpeted box. I held the waist at the right height and he made some chalk marks at the back. Then he knelt down on the floor. "Hold them just like that," he said with his mouth full of pins. "Just a little break in the trouser, very smart for a young man," he said half to himself and marked the measurements on a pad.

"Now the waistcoat." He put the vest on me and adjusted the back strap. "We'll take a little out on the sides. Some of my customers would love to have a waist like yours, believe me." He pinned the vest sides and then had me take it off and put on the jacket. I hardly recognized myself in the mirror. Rine adjusted the jacket lapels and stood back. "Beautiful. A classic suit, wonderful flannel. We'll lift the collar a bit, lower this sleeve a quarter-inch, that should be perfect." He really loved his work. "There. We can have it ready tomorrow afternoon."

"Thank you." I was sorry to take the suit off. When I put on my old brown jacket, it looked stretched and shapeless. Rine hung up the suit carefully, opened the cash drawer, and handed me a ten-dollar bill. "At twenty percent discount the suit is forty dollars. I'd rather have everything evened up."

"Thank you, I would too." I gave him back his IOU and he tore it up.

"You know, you have good taste for a person your age. I hope that one day you'll spend some of your own money on our clothes."

"I hope so too." I meant it; I was glad to have bought the suit.

"You finished?" Tony asked, and moved toward the door. When we were almost there, Rine called, "Uh, boys? I was wondering if you'd like to make another bet." I couldn't believe my ears. We looked at each other, then at Rine. He licked his lips. "A bet on the whole Series."

"On the whole Series," Tony repeated.

"Sure," Rine said, sounding more confident. "It's two to two, it could go either way now." I could read it on his face: He wanted to make up their losses and surprise Whitworth. We walked back to the counter. "Who do you want?" Tony asked.

"Well, let's see, it's even now," Rine said, looking at a suit rack. I realized that he wasn't talking to us, he was thinking out loud. "Two for the Yanks and two for the Giants. So it's the Yanks's turn next and if they take three they'll probably take five. And the papers say that the team that loses the first two games loses the Series." He turned to us. "We'll take the Yanks. That's fair, isn't it? You've already won a lot from us, so we should get the choice."

"How much?" Tony asked.

"Two hundred?"

That would cover their losses and then some, I thought. Tony looked at me questioningly. "I'm game if you are."

"Okay, two hundred bucks then."

"We better write this one down," I said. I wrote out two dated copies of the bet on Rine & Whitworth sales slips and we all signed them. Then we shook hands. "We'll see you later," Tony said.

"And don't forget, the suit will be ready late Tuesday

afternoon." I looked back from outside and saw Rine mimicking Babe Ruth's left-handed stance in the back of the store. Swish! he swung a yardstick and batted a pincushion across the room. It was funny; in the dim light he did look a little like Ruth.

Everybody, including me, expected the Babe to hit more homers, but when he came up that afternoon in the first inning of the fifth game he looked like a war casualty. He had bandages on his left elbow and wrist, and he was limping badly. The papers said that the abscess on his left elbow was open and draining, that both legs were bandaged to the hips, and that he had a severe charley horse. Art Nehf had already eliminated the first two Yankee batters, and he threw Ruth a series of perfectly timed sucker balls and struck him out. When the Giants came up against Waite Hoyt in the first they made a couple of outs and then loaded the bases. Before the third out George Kelly singled to center field and scored Dave Bancroft. One nothing; we were off to a good start.

The Yankees caught up in the third inning when Elmer Miller, the center fielder, hit a sacrifice fly to left field and scored Bob Meusel. Well, one to one isn't hopeless, I thought, but the old nervousness was back. Babe Ruth led off in the fourth inning. A lot of people stood up to watch him, hoping for a homer. He surprised everyone in the Polo Grounds, especially Art Nehf and catcher Earl Smith, when he laid down a tiny bunt along the third base line and beat it to first. Smith looked furious, but Judge Landis's fine must have worked, because he kept quiet. Two hundred bucks was a huge fine, I thought. Then I remembered that it was the same as our bet.

I had been feeling cocky because of our record so far and

Tony's confidence that the Giants would win the Series. I began to feel less secure when Bob Meusel doubled and scored Ruth. The Babe nearly collapsed as he crossed the plate, and several teammates helped him to the dugout. The next batter, Wally Pipp, grounded to second, and Meusel made it to third base. "Damn, they'll sacrifice," Tony said, and he was right. Aaron Ward hit a high fly to center field and Meusel scored easily after the catch. The Yankees led 3 to 1. "Don't worry," Tony said. "Ruth's probably out of the game, and we'll get 'em later."

To our amazement Ruth walked shakily to left field at the beginning of the fifth. I kept waiting for the Giants' late-inning rally. Art Nehf pitched great ball, retiring batters one-two-three, but so did Waite Hoyt. There was no rally, in fact there was no score on either side for the last five innings, and the game ended with the same score, Yankees 3, Giants 1. "That's three to two in the Series," I reminded Tony.

"Quit worrying. We're doing great so far, right?"

When we came back to the hotel there was a package of laundry on the bureau. My knickers and jacket were permanently rumpled, but I felt like a swell having beautiful clean shirts to wear every day. New clothes and thirty-five dollars in cash besides! I realized that tomorrow it would be a week since I came to New York. It was so easy to get used to the Plaza that I had completely lost track of time. On an impulse I picked up the telephone and called home. I was surprised when my father answered. "Hello, Poppa."

"Sol!" He actually sounded glad to hear from me for a second. Then his regular tone came back. "You come home now."

"I told you, Poppa, I have to stay with the Fabulous Fifty. How are you, how's Momma, how are Elena and Georgio?"

"Okay. You can eat?"

"It's all taken care of, Poppa, the newspaper pays for everything."

I could almost hear him shaking his head like it wasn't right. "You have money still?"

"I have some money, Poppa, don't worry."

"The six dollars from Momma?"

"It's enough, Poppa. Besides, I have more than that." I was sorry the moment I said it.

"How you have more money?" His tone was angry.

"We sold some tickets for some of it, and the rest I won." I waited for the outburst; only grown-up Greek men gambled.

There was a long silence. *"Ti?"*

"I told you, I won most of it. Tony and I bet on the baseball games."

There was another silence. *"Pohso?"*

"All together I made eighty-five dollars. I won seventy, but I used fifty of it to buy new clothes, so I only have thirty-five left."

"Evthomeenda dollaria? You win seventy dollars?"

"Yes, Poppa."

"Theos." I heard my mother ask him if anything was wrong. *"Eeneh endahksee,"* he told her impatiently; everything's fine.

"Pohssa ekhases?"

"I haven't lost anything."

"Theos," he said again; he sounded dazed. "I talk when you come home. Here is Momma."

"Hello, Momma. Don't worry about my clothes, I have some new ones."

"You're all right?"

"I'm fine. Did you call the principal?"

"*Neh,* we called. I don't know."

"I'll straighten it out when I come home. You take care, all right? Say hello to Elena and Georgios for me."

"*Kherete.*" She sounded dazed too.

"Was your old man mad?" Tony asked.

"No, he wasn't. I can't figure it out. Maybe he won some bets himself."

"Does he bet a lot?"

"All the time."

"Yeah, my old man too. I guess they all do."

RUTH OUT OF GAME BY DOCTOR'S ORDERS, the front page of the *New York Times* said next morning. On top of the infected abscess and his other injuries, he had wrenched his knee badly in the fifth game. Chick Fewster would be playing left field for the Yankees that afternoon, and the sportswriters doubted that Ruth would play in the Series again.

I was awed when the Babe himself appeared right below us in street clothes before the game began. He stood in the aisle of the front boxes chatting with friends. "Look at that," I said to Tony, "his arm is bandaged over his suit jacket." Tony didn't answer, and when I turned around he wasn't in the box. A moment later I saw him slip through the group around Ruth and hold out his hand. Ruth smiled and shook hands with him. One of the photographers asked for a picture, and Ruth put his hand on Tony's shoulder and they both grinned at the camera. Then Tony took out his program, and Ruth took out a pen. I was full of envy; why didn't I have nerve like that? In a few minutes Ruth sat down with his wife and Tony came back to our seats flushed with triumph. "Look at this!" His program was autographed, "Best of luck to Tony Ammanati, Babe Ruth." "I told ya I'd get to meet him." All the Fabulous Fifty members wanted to see the autograph, and Tony showed it off until the first pitch.

I worried that the papers were right about the Series, even without Ruth. The Yankees fielded a pitcher named Harry Harper, and after walking George Burns he settled down and retired the Giants in order. When the Yanks came to bat, Fred Toney got off to a bad start by walking Chick Fewster and giving up singles to Elmer Miller and Bob Meusel that scored Fewster. Toney stopped Roger Peckinpaugh and Wally Pipp, but then Aaron Ward hit a long drive to center field that let both Miller and Meusel score. Before we knew it the Yanks were ahead 3 to 0, and McGraw had to send in Jesse Barnes to get the third out.

Harper walked George Kelly, the first Giants batter in the second inning. Irish Meusel looked grim when he came to bat, and he drilled Harper's first good pitch into the right field grandstand for a two-run homer. "Yayyy!" we screamed like maniacs. You could tell the Giants were angry. Johnny Rawlings took a mighty cut and flied out to deep center field. Then the catcher, Frank Snyder, came up and walloped another homer into the left field bleachers. That was it for Harper; Bob Shawkey came in to pitch for the Yankees and cleaned up the inning without another run.

Jesse Barnes seemed to have everything under control

when he struck out Wally Schang on fastballs. The next Yankee batter was the new pitcher, trying to save his own game. Shawkey singled to left field, and behind him came Ruth's replacement, Chick Fewster. A few people booed Fewster, but he walked up to the plate and hit a two-run homer into the same spot as Frank Snyder. Barnes pulled it together again, and the inning ended Yankees 5, Giants 3. Sam looked through his little pocket book of statistics. "Ah, I thought so," he said. "Three home runs in one inning is a new World Series record."

"I don't know if I can stand a whole game of this," Jim Hilferty said. I felt the same way. Even though the Giants were losing, the no-score third inning was a welcome break from the excitement.

It also seemed to break the Yankees's spirit. Chick Fewster was playing good ball, but he just wasn't the same as Babe Ruth. In the fourth inning the Giants walked over Shawkey: Frank Snyder, Jesse Barnes, and George Burns singled one after another, and then Dave Bancroft hit a line drive to left field and drove in Snyder and Barnes. Frankie Frisch hit a single that forced Bancroft, and promptly stole second to make up for it. Shawkey took a deep breath and struck out Ross Youngs, but then George Kelly hit a long drive to right field that scored Burns and Frisch. It looked like the start of another rally until Kelly slipped when he tried to steal second and was thrown out. The Giants were ahead 7 to 5. Sam was perspiring even though it was chilly. He mopped his face and grinned at me. "This is worth those nine thousand coupons and then some."

Jesse Barnes bore down and struck out three Yankee batters in the bottom of the fourth. After the Giants rally I expected Huggins to pull Shawkey, but he came back in the fifth inning and kept the Giants bottled up. Barnes was just as tight; he fanned the first two Yankee batters, and then threw a spinner that Roger Peckinpaugh popped up for the third out. The Giants hit Shawkey again in the sixth inning, but only Frankie Frisch was left on base after the second out. By this time Jim Hilferty had become a great Frisch fan. "Go Frankie!" he yelled, and when George Kelly hit a long single to center field Frankie went, all the way home. That made it Giants 8, Yankees 5.

Even though Bob Shawkey retired the Giants in order for the next two innings, Huggins sent in Bill Piercy in the ninth. Jesse Barnes got more consistent as the game drew to a close. In the last half of the ninth inning he threw the same grooved low pitches to Chick Fewster, Roger Peckinpaugh, and Elmer Miller, and one after another they popped up to second base like windup toys. Johnny Rawlings hardly had to move; he just stood there and caught three outs in a row. We were sort of back where we started. Tuesday, October 11, 1921: With six games played the World Series was tied up, three games to three.

CHAPTER 31

After the game Tony and I hurried over to Rine & Whitworth to pick up my suit. I figured that I'd get to wear it for at least a couple of days. There were some customers in the store and we waited outside until they left. Rine intercepted us at the door, winking furiously. "Well, hi boys!" Whitworth came up behind him. "Oh, it's you two again. Got any bets today?" Rine gave us a warning look.

"Well, maybe," I said.

"I hope they win."

"I'm here to pick up my suit."

"I know," Whitworth clipped. "He'll take care of it."

"Don't mind him," Rine said after Whitworth went into the back office. "He gets crabby sometimes. He's very high-strung." He had me try on the whole suit. None of us were prepared for the full effect. "Lovely," Rine said. Tony looked me up and down. "That is really spiffy, sport. Maybe I should get one like that too." I knew he wouldn't; money meant more to him than anything. And if we lost our bet, where would we get that much money?

I couldn't bear to change back into my old clothes. Rine put them in a bag; and when I walked by Joe Morello in the hotel lobby, he didn't even recognize me. Tony gave me the idea of having my old jacket and knickers cleaned by the Plaza's overnight service. It was a perfect day to have new clothes, because there was a Fabulous Fifty banquet that night at the hotel. I wore the blue suit, a clean shirt, and my two-dollar tie, and when I came into the dining room Mrs. Mendel stopped me and told me I looked handsome. "Thank you, ma'am." I felt myself blushing. *"Kineahora,"* she said. "I wouldn't mind having a son like you." She sat down at the head table with Mrs. Markevich and Harry Johnson and the other assistants. Both women were wearing corsages. "What's *kineahora* mean?" I whispered to Tony.

"Beats me. It must be some Jewish word." I figured I would ask Hymie when we got home. We sat with Sam and Jim Hilferty, and Joe Morello and two of his Mafia buddies from Strawberry Mansion sat across from us. Everyone was talking about the Series. Harry Johnson stood up and tapped a spoon on a glass. "Welcome, Fabulous Fifty, and special personal greetings from Mr. Summerhill, the publisher of the *Clarion*. Are you having a good time?" Someone started to clap and we gave Harry a long round of applause. "That's what we like to hear. You may have thought it was funny when I called you a big happy family last week on the roof of the *Clarion* building, but you see, I was right." There was another round of applause.

"You can understand that with a nine-game World Series we weren't sure when it would be over, so we scheduled the banquet for tonight. We have some nice surprises for you, but first I want to mention a few missing colleagues. You may have heard that Marvin Black, one of our assistants, had an appendicitis attack. Well, Marvin is a little lighter, but he's mending perfectly and went home from the hospital today. Ah, youth." Everybody laughed. "We're also short two winners tonight. Mr. Leonard returned to Philadelphia because of, ah, indisposition, and Jim Cox, whom many of us had grown to like very much, had to go home because his son has the flu."

There was a murmur of concern. "Poor guy," Joe Morello said. In 1921 flu didn't mean a bad cold, it meant influenza, a terrible disease that killed thousands of people every year. "My daughter Angie lost her first baby in the '18 epidemic," Morello said. "A beautiful grandson." One of his friends put a hand on his arm. Morello wiped his eyes with a napkin. "Sorry," he said.

"I'll be glad to give Jim's address to anyone who'd like to keep in touch with him," Harry continued. "Now, as I said, we have some surprises for you, but if you were as excited as I was during today's game, you're probably in the mood for dinner first and surprises later, right?"

"Right!" Sam answered him, and we all laughed.

"That's what I thought. The Plaza's chef has made a grand banquet for us, and I hope you all enjoy it." We clapped some more, Harry sat down, and the waiters brought the first course. It was a big silver plate with six shells nested in coarse salt. Each shell was mounded with brown bread crumbs and decorated with a red letter Y. "What is it?" I asked.

"Read the menu," Sam said. I opened the red, white, and blue folder: *Fabulous Fifty Banquet, Tuesday, October 11, 1921.* The first course was called *Clams Yankee.* I recognized the bread crumbs and I could smell bacon, but I wasn't sure about the rest. "What's the red stuff?" I asked Sam.

"Pimiento," he answered, chewing. Three of his shells were empty already. I wanted to try a little bite, but it was all one piece. I put it in my mouth; it tasted strange, but I couldn't think of a way to get rid of it, so I chewed it up and ate it anyway. By the third one it didn't taste so strange. "That was good," Morello said, "but I sure could use a nice glass of wine."

Like magic a waiter appeared and began pouring what looked like ginger ale in our glasses. "What's that?" I asked him.

"Don't worry, kid, it ain't champagne," Morello said.

"It's sparkling catawba grape juice, sir," the waiter answered. I took a sip; it was sweet and the bubbles went up my nose. "Pooey," Morello said. "That damn Prohibition is the dumbest law they ever passed. What's wrong with a little glass of vino with dinner?"

"I agree," Sam said. "Prohibition is the misconceived idea of a bunch of joyless stringbeans."

"Like that Leonard," Jim said. "Did you ever see such a sour guy? I never saw him crack a smile once. I know he's in a wheelchair, but so is my uncle Roy, and he keeps us in stitches."

"Harry told me that he hated the trip," Sam said. "He thought we were a bunch of crude rowdies."

"T.S., huh?" Morello said. "We can do without him."

The waiters took the silver dishes away—I had eaten all the clams without thinking—and brought soup plates. *Crème Géant,* the menu said. It was chicken soup, I think, and it had cream in it and tiny bits of ham and parsley, and little baked letter *G*'s floating on top. "Delicious," Jim said. "Good for what ails you."

Next there was *Sole Amérique,* fish in a pastry crust with a little baseball diamond outlined on it, and *Poulet Nationale,* chicken with potatoes carved like little baseballs and carrots made into bats. "Who does this stuff?" I asked Sam. "I mean carving the food into fancy shapes."

"Apprentices, kids who want to be chefs. They start out peeling vegetables and work their way up through the kitchen."

Then we had what I thought was dessert, raspberry ice, but Sam said it was a sorbet to cleanse your palate before the next course. The waiters took away our glasses and filled new ones with sparkling red grape juice, and brought *Boeuf Rôti Series du Monde,* roast beef surrounded with little bread fielders' gloves and thin slices of turnip, Sam said, in the shape of home plate. It was good, but I was completely stuffed. "How can people eat this much for dinner?"

"It's easy," Tony said. He had cleaned the last three courses off his plate in record time; I didn't know where he was putting it. "There are people that eat this way every night," Sam said, and I could tell that he wished he were one of them. Morello sat back and burped. "Good food, though, huh, kid? Don't worry, you'll have room for dessert."

The waiters cleared everything off and brought coffee cups and saucers. They poured the coffee from silver pitchers, and it smelled and tasted wonderful. "And now," Harry Johnson announced, "The pièce de résistance!" The room lights dimmed, and two men carried in a huge silver platter with a white model of the Polo Grounds on it. There were pennants flying from the flagpoles on the roof and blue flames all over it. They carried it around the tables so we could admire it. "How about that?" Harry said, and everyone applauded. I thought it was a nifty model, and I wondered if they carried it past everybody's table during the World Series. The room lights went on again, and I waited for them to take away the Polo Grounds and bring dessert. I was astonished when the headwaiter took a big knife and cut off a piece of the grandstand and put it on a plate. Another waiter put the plate in front of Mrs. Markevich.

"You mean we're going to *eat* it?" I said, much too loud, and the whole room burst out laughing. I blushed flaming red.

"It's Baked Alaska, Sol," Sam said. Baked Alaska sounded just as strange as edible Polo Grounds. A waiter brought me a big piece with home plate on it. I cut off a bite while everybody around me watched. The outside was meringue still warm from the oven, there was cake underneath, and in the middle was ice cream! It was like magic. "Well, what do you think?" Sam asked.

"It's wonderful. How do they keep the ice cream from melting?"

"Don't worry about it, just enjoy it." Like he said, this trip was worth all the coupons.

After dessert most of the men lit cigars. Joe Morello offered me one, but I remembered Mark getting sick after smoking one of his father's cigars at a club meeting. "No, thank you," I told him.

"How about me?" Tony asked.

Morello looked him over. "You gotta put on a few pounds yet. Besides, your old man would get after me."

The waiters put little dishes of mints around the table,

and Harry Johnson stood up and asked, "Did everyone have enough to eat?"

There were loud groans and cheers. "That's good. I see the boys didn't leave any of the infield." Everyone looked over and laughed. Harry went on to say what a nice group we were and how much the *Clarion* staff enjoyed working with us. "Up to now it was easy, but now we have some heavy work, eh, Dan?"

Dan smiled and took a cloth cover off a stack of cartons against the wall behind Harry and brought one of the cartons to the table. "You'll remember," Harry said, "that besides this splendid trip there were going to be prizes awarded to the Fabulous Fifty. Well, the number of companies that wanted to be represented absolutely astounded us. I wish that some of these items had arrived a little earlier, but you'll still get some use out of them."

He reached into the carton and took out a box camera. "This is a present for each of you from the Eastman company, a genuine Kodak, complete with two rolls of film and an instruction book." There was a burst of applause. "I knew you'd like that," Harry said, "but if you applaud each prize we'll be here till midnight. In case you want to write down the names of the people in your snapshots—" he reached into the box and took out a leather case—"the Parker Pen Company has given each of you a gold-filled pen-and-pencil set. They say Fabulous Fifty right on the barrel. In fact, you'd have to be an octopus to use everything you're getting to write with." There was a Sheaffer pen-and-pencil set, there were mechanical pencils from six different companies, and there were miniature bridge pencils in two sets of Fabulous Fifty playing cards.

"This is the other thing besides the camera we hoped to have last week." Harry held up a small pair of field glasses. "Anyway, you'll get to use them for at least two and maybe three games." I nudged Tony, and he grinned at me; the guys were going to love this stuff. There were three cigarette lighters and five different key rings. All of them said Fabulous Fifty someplace or other; we were going to be marked for life. "Now you may want to be sure you get up in time for tomorrow's game." Harry chuckled and held up an alarm clock. "That reminds me of work," Jim Hilferty called.

"Me too," Harry said. "But if it's too bulky we have something else." He held up a box that looked like another pen set. When he opened it, there was a murmur of surprise. "That's right," Harry said, "a genuine Elgin wristwatch for everyone here. A hundred percent American made."

"Gorgeous," Mrs. Mendel said. She started to clap and we all joined in.

"Thank you," Harry said. "But we have to move along. Now believe it or not, you also have—" he took out another case—"a second fine wristwatch, made by Benrus."

"This is really something," Sam said. "I had forgotten about this part."

Harry went on and on. There was a pocket watch, three different Fabulous Fifty pocketknives, a brush-and-comb set, baseball caps, and wallets. There was even a box of cigars. "Now, we weren't sure whether we'd have any ladies," Harry said, "and you can see that many of these prizes are, well, masculine." He signaled to Dan and an assistant put large gift-wrapped boxes in front of Mrs. Markevich and Mrs. Mendel. "Go ahead, ladies, open them." Inside each box was a tray with a big matching dressing set, a brush and comb and hand mirror and buttonhook, and little boxes for powder and hairpins and stuff. It was a kind of pearly green color, and both women oohed and aahed over it. We all clapped, but personally I wouldn't have wanted anything like that on my bureau.

Harry was reaching into the bottom of the box. He came up with a book about baseball, a Fabulous Fifty tie, a perpetual calendar, a belt with a Fabulous Fifty buckle, and the framed picture that was taken on the roof of the *Clarion* building the day we left. It seemed like months ago. "Now we know you're thinking, 'This is very nice, but how am I going to cart all that stuff home?'" Dan brought over a flat box, and Harry opened it and plumped up a canvas overnight bag like athletes used, with FABULOUS FIFTY 1921 printed on both sides.

"Boy, they really thought of everything," Sam said. He started clapping and the applause grew and grew. Harry made Dan and the other assistants stand up, and we kept on clapping until he started to blush himself. Until it happened, I wouldn't have thought it was possible.

CHAPTER 32

Between the stuff I had won from Rine & Whitworth and the Fabulous Fifty prizes, my bureau drawers were getting pretty full. When I put on my cleaned and pressed jacket and knickers Wednesday morning they looked like different clothes. That was October 12, Columbus Day, and Mrs. Mendel told us at breakfast it was also Yom Kippur, the biggest Jewish holiday. She said that while she wasn't religious, she wasn't going to the game that day. I tried to take my mind off our bet by reading the baseball book they gave us at the banquet, but I left the hotel in the same nervous state as at the beginning of the Series.

The pitchers for the seventh game were the same as on the first day: Phil Douglas versus Carl Mays. It was so cold and windy at the Polo Grounds that I wondered how they stayed warm between pitches. I drank hot chocolate and sat on my hands through the first few innings. There were probably many people besides us who were worried about the tiebreaker, because the crowd looked like the biggest yet.

The game was a pitchers' duel right from the start. There was no score in the first inning, and we watched every pitch as if it was the last one of the game. In the top of the second inning the Yanks started a rally. Wally Pipp, the first man up, hit a double to left field. Aaron Ward sacrificed him to third base, and then Mike McNally hit a single to right field that scored Pipp. Douglas clamped the lid on again, the next two batters hit right into Johnny Rawlings's glove at second base, and it was Yankees 1, Giants 0.

The Giants' second-inning batting didn't look so good. George Kelly struck out, and Irish Meusel and Johnny Rawlings each hit grounders to third. Mike McNally, the Yankee third baseman, stopped both balls smartly and threw the runners out at first. He had a peculiar throw; he would leap up in the air when he pegged the ball across the diamond. After the second throw he winced and grabbed his right arm. Miller Huggins met him halfway to the dugout; McNally tried to move his arm and shook his head.

Even though Chick Fewster and Roger Peckinpaugh singled, the Yanks couldn't score in the top of the third, and when they took the field again Frank Baker was playing third base instead of McNally. I knew about "Home Run Baker" from Philadelphia. He got his nickname when he hit two homers for the Athletics in the 1911 World Series. He was a solid hitter but a slow runner.

George Burns's double was the only hit the Giants made in their third turn at bat, and then Douglas retired the Yanks in order in the top of the fourth. When the Giants came up in the bottom of the inning Frankie Frisch grounded to the pitcher, but Ross Youngs hit a hard infield single and then stole second base. Tony and I stood up and yelled "Go Giants!" George Kelly must not have heard us, because he struck out. "C'mon, c'mon, you still got a chance," Tony said, and sure enough Irish Meusel hit a long single to center field and Youngs scored. Mays was as tough as Douglas; he cracked down on Johnny Rawlings for the third out, and the game stayed tied at 1 to 1 for the next two innings.

"This is pretty slow after yesterday," Sam complained at the seventh-inning stretch. It wasn't a slow game if you liked good pitching, but there wasn't much slugging to watch. Jim Hilferty was disgusted when Irish Meusel fanned to make the Giants' second out in the bottom of the seventh. Then Johnny Rawlings hit a ground ball to second that looked like an easy out. Aaron Ward was caught off guard, fumbled it, and Rawlings made it to first. Frank Snyder, the Giants' catcher, was up next. I had been surprised to read in the morning paper that he had the highest batting average of any player in the Series, even higher than Babe Ruth's. He showed why when he smacked a pitch from Mays into left center field for a clean double and scored Rawlings. "Hot dog!" Tony crowed, "now we're goin'."

We weren't going far, because Phil Douglas struck out; just far enough. Both pitchers kept the pressure on for the whole nine innings, and we stayed hypnotized while dark rain clouds gathered overhead. There wasn't much cheering at the end, but it was Giants 2, Yankees 1. We were ahead! I was so cold and tired when we came back to the hotel that I laid down and fell sound asleep.

"Hey, you coming to dinner?"

"Huh?"

"It's six o'clock. You slept almost two hours."

"Is that right?" I opened my eyes a crack and shut them again. Tony was sitting on the edge of my bed. "I feel like I could sleep all night."

"C'mon, we're goin' to a Chinese restaurant tonight."

"Okay, I'm coming." I rolled over, sat up, and realized that what I really wanted to do was get undressed and go to sleep. "Listen, Tony, I'm dead tired. I think I'll skip the restaurant."

"Yeah?" He looked at me worriedly. "You okay?"

"Sure, I'm just tired. I really need some sleep."

"Okay, I'll tell them that." He went into the bathroom to wash, and I took my clothes off and slipped under the covers. I could hear the wind howling outside and knew it was the right decision. I lay there feeling warm and cozy and listening to the small noises Tony made getting dressed. "Hey, do you think the guys will mind if I wear one of the wristwatches tonight?" he asked.

"I don't think so. There's more than enough to go around anyway. Dan told me there's a whole batch of presents that they didn't bring to New York."

"Those guys are gonna love it." He put the watch on and looked at himself in the mirror. "I need some long pants."

"Have a good dinner."

"I will. See you later." He turned the lights out and shut the door.

It was very quiet after he left. I could hear faint traffic noises, the wind outside, and once in a while the footsteps of people walking down the hall. I felt even more secure than I did in my bedroom at home. I guess I never thought about that at home. The sixth floor of the Plaza was the highest place I had ever slept, and the hotel bed was firm and level. Mine—it was really Elena's old one—sagged in the middle as if people had been sleeping in it for a long time. My uncle Angelos liked to joke about people wearing out the bed.

I wondered if Elena had ever made love with Mark, or

with anyone. I wished that I could ask her. She would like it here, I thought. She was a sweet sister, and I knew she was proud of me for winning the Fabulous Fifty contest and the Foote School math prize. Sometime I would have to tell her about Cissie, was the last thing I thought of before I fell asleep.

Thursday morning's papers said that the Series gate receipts had broken all records: $804,781. "That's nearly a million dollars!" Tony said, as if he had a vision of the Virgin Mary. "What are the odds for today?" I asked him.

"It says three and a half to one on the Giants, and there's about a hundred thousand bucks on the game." Two hundred of that is ours, I thought. How did the papers know how much people were betting? We hadn't told anyone. There were a lot of things I didn't understand. "It says it's going to be cold again today," Tony said. I noticed that he had learned how to hold the paper like a professional; he even had some of Sam Hart's expressions when he read the news.

A brisk wind was whipping across the Polo Grounds when we arrived, and I wished I had a Rine & Whitworth sweater under my jacket. "See the umpire's name?" Jim Hilferty asked. I looked at the program: *O. Chill.* "Is that a joke?"

"Nope, but I think he's running the game and the weather too." He called over a vendor and bought hot chocolates for us. On Wednesday Judge Landis had flipped a coin to decide which team would be "at home" if they played a ninth game on Friday, and the Giants won, which meant they would bat last. Today the Yankees had the last turn and they were pinning their hopes on Waite Hoyt. In the first inning he was a little shaky, and so were his teammates.

Not that the Giants were doing much to cheer about. George Burns, the first batter, grounded out to third base. Hoyt walked Dave Bancroft, and then Frankie Frisch hit a short foul to Wally Pipp at first. "Darn," Jim Hilferty said, "I have a little bet on them today."

Sam looked surprised. "I didn't know you were a betting man."

"I'm not usually, and Alice doesn't like it, but I thought ten bucks just this once. You don't get to the World Series every year, right, boys?"

"Right," we chorused and looked at each other.

Ross Youngs was up next, and to our surprise Hoyt walked him, advancing Bancroft to second base. George Kelly, the Giants' big first baseman came to the plate swinging his bat purposefully. Tony checked the program. "He's only hittin' two thirty-three. Ah, nuts." Kelly hit a ground ball straight to Roger Peckinpaugh at shortstop, but as Peckinpaugh bent to scoop it up, it bounced between his legs into the outfield. By the time he recovered it Kelly was safe on first and Bancroft had scored the first run of the game. Tony slapped me on the back. "Another two-out rally!" There were still two men on base and Irish Meusel was up. "A double, let's have a double," Tony breathed. Hoyt knew just what he was doing. He sent Meusel a low sucker ball that Meusel grounded right back to him, and that was that. Giants 1, Yankees 0.

"Well, it's better than nothing," Jim said to Sam.

"Right. Maybe we'll have another slugging match like the third game."

It was Art Nehf's turn to keep Sam waiting. He struck Chick Fewster out, but then he walked Roger Peckinpaugh, and he was in the same place Hoyt had been a few minutes earlier. It got worse when Elmer Miller singled to right field, sending Peckinpaugh to second base. Bob Meusel came up next. The pressure was on, and Nehf showed it by throwing a wild pitch over Frank Snyder's head. Miller and Peckinpaugh went to second and third on that, and Snyder came out to have a little talk with Nehf. Nehf walked calmly back to the mound chewing his tobacco, wound up, and sent Bob Meusel a duplicate of the ball his brother Irish had muffed. Meusel popped up short to George Kelly at first base, and Kelly had the ball to home plate in an instant. Nobody moved. "Two outs," Jim said. We were riveted on the field. Wally Pipp was up next. Nehf read Snyder's signals carefully, wound up his limber left arm, and struck Pipp out.

"Whew," Jim said. "That's what I call bearing down in the clutch."

"That's what they pay them for," Sam said. We knew he liked to see homers more than strikeouts, but it wasn't his day. The first inning set the pattern for half the game: Every time either team had a man in scoring position, the other pitcher blocked the run. In the top of the second Johnny Rawlings hit a solid double and then was thrown out at the plate by Roger Peckinpaugh. Hoyt gave up no hits in the Giants' half of the third inning, and Peckinpaugh hit into a double play to end the Yankees' third turn at bat. In the fourth inning the Yankees, fighting for survival, loaded the bases with two outs. Nehf bore down again and Wally Schang flied out to center field to end the inning scoreless. I was getting more and more tense.

"Gosh, this is worse than the seventh game," Sam said. I was beginning to think that he had a secret bet on the Yankees, and that all his talk about hits was just a cover-up. As the game went on, the pitchers seemed to get stronger and the batters weaker. There was only one hit by either side in the fifth, sixth, and seventh innings, and in the eighth both teams were retired in order, with Hoyt and Nehf each striking out one batter. The Giants' last chance to increase their one-run lead was the top of the ninth. The first man up was Frank Snyder, hitting .369. "Let's go, Frankie," Tony murmured. Snyder was trying too hard; he took a mighty, mistimed cut and grounded out to Frank Baker at third base. "Aw, Frankie," Jim said. Tony looked worried because Art Nehf was next and Tony had no faith in the hitting abilities of pitchers. His instinct was right again. Nehf went down swinging. Two outs! Hoyt was right in the groove. He tempted George Burns into a slow grounder back to the mound, and it was up to the Yanks to save their last chance for the Series. My stomach was churning.

Wally Pipp was the next man in the Yankee lineup, but all twenty-five thousand people at the Polo Grounds stood up when Babe Ruth limped into the batter's box to pinch hit. His arm was heavily bandaged and he looked worn, but you could never tell. Nehf sized him up and pitched carefully. Ruth hit a slow, sad grounder to George Kelly at first base. Kelly tagged the base and Ruth slowly ran it out, turned around, and limped back to the dugout. You could feel the disappointment in the stadium. Everyone sat down with a sort of sigh.

The strain showed on Nehf, because he walked Aaron Ward, the next man up. The third batter was Frank Baker.

"Uh oh," Tony said, "you remember his nickname?"

"Of course," I said, annoyed to be reminded. A Yankee home run with a man on base was the last thing we needed now. Nehf let up for only one pitch, but it was enough for Baker. He slammed a line drive toward right field that looked like a sure double and Ward took off for second like a scared rabbit. We were all on our feet. Suddenly from out of nowhere Johnny Rawlings, the Giants second baseman, came racing desperately toward the ball. He threw himself at it, stopped it near the edge of the right field grass, and sprawled full-length on his face. In a split second he bounced up, turned, and threw out the slow-running Baker at first. The crowd roared. Ward, on his way to third, hesitated, and George Kelly rifled a throw from first base to Frankie Frisch at third and cut him off. Three outs. The Series was over. Just like that. *The Series was over!* "We won! We won!" Tony screamed, and threw his arms around my neck. "Yayyy, Giants!!" we shouted, and Frankie Frisch heard us down on the field. He turned around, held up his hands together, and grinned right at us. "Well, how about that," Jim said. "I won my bet."

Tony winked at me. Oh boy, I thought, oh boy. When we got back to the hotel, the lobby was packed with fans listening to the radio recap on WJZ. It was the biggest-money World Series ever, the announcer said: Each member of the winning team would receive $5,265, and each loser $3,510. Even the losers' shares sounded big to me. "C'mon," Tony said, "let's go get ours."

Rine's face was as white as his shirt when we walked in. "You guys back again?" Whitworth said.

"Uh, Tom," Rine began. Whitworth looked at him

suspiciously. Rine swallowed and came out with it fast: "I-made-another-bet-I-meant-to-win-it-all-back-so-we-wouldn't-lose-so-much."

"You made another bet," Whitworth said slowly. "And?"

"And—well, we lost."

"*We* lost? I didn't make any bet."

"I made it for both of us."

"In writing," I said.

"Right," Tony said. "In writing."

"In writing," Whitworth repeated dully. "May I see it, please?"

Rine swallowed again, took out his wallet, and unfolded his copy of the bet. Whitworth read my Foote School legal language. "Oh," he said, "you lost two hundred dollars. *Two hundred dollars!*" he shouted. I was scared; I thought maybe he was going to kill Rine. He balled up the paper and threw it on the floor.

"We have another copy," I said.

Rine ran to the front door. I thought he was going to slip out, but he shut and locked it and pulled down the shade. "Two hundred dollars!" Whitworth shouted again. He began to pace back and forth like a caged animal. His eyes were wide; he looked right through Tony and me. We edged behind a counter. He picked up a yardstick and began to swing it wildly. It broke against a showcase and he dropped it. He jerked his tie loose, pulling until he tore it. Then he threw all the socks from their case out onto the floor, scrabbling at them and panting like a dog. Tony and I stood frozen, watching him. I glanced at Rine; he looked pale but not especially frightened. Whitworth pulled his shirt open, ripping the buttons off it. "Two hundred dollars," he whispered. Then he went into the back room.

Rine motioned to us to be quiet. He tiptoed around the shop, picked up the buttons and pieces of yardstick and dropped them into a wastebasket. Tony and I helped him pile the socks back in the case. Then, still silent, he went back to the door and hung a sign behind the shade: CLOSED.

When Whitworth came out of the back room a few minutes later you couldn't have told from his appearance that anything had happened. He was wearing a new shirt and tie and his hair was freshly brilliantined. He looked around the shop. "I'm sorry about that," he said.

Neither of us knew what to say. I had never seen anything like it before. "Maybe it'll be a lesson to us," Whitworth said. "I'll level with you. We can't pay you in cash. We can't spare that much cash until after Christmas, and I presume you don't want to wait that long."

Tony and I looked at each other. "That's true," I said.

"We'll give you fifty bucks in cash if you'll take the rest in trade. Right now."

I looked at Tony. He shrugged. "Okay," he said.

It was some afternoon. I chose a dark red sweater—maroon, Rine called it—two pairs of long flannel pants, two more shirts, a new belt, scarves for my mom and Elena, a tie for my dad, a pocketknife for Georgio, and a suitcase to carry everything in. I knew what Tony wanted: long pants. "Odd trousers," Rine called them, and Tony bought four pairs. He got a jacket, some shirts and ties, a billfold, and presents for his mom and dad. Rine was as patient with us as if we were buying the stuff with our own money. He was upset that we wouldn't leave the pants to be cuffed, but we thought it would be better to get it over with. He put the gift ties in boxes, like we were old customers.

Even Whitworth mellowed toward the end and helped Tony pick out a nice-looking jacket. When we were finished, I packed everything in my suitcase, and Rine wrapped Tony's stuff to go back to the hotel. Then we tore up the IOUs and shook hands, and Tony and I left Rine & Whitworth for the last time.

CHAPTER 33

We came back to the Plaza at six-thirty and found that we had missed a meeting of the Fabulous Fifty. There was a note under our door to call Harry or Dan. We called Dan, and he came up to the room. It turned out that the *Clarion* had overnight reservations for us, but if we liked we could go back to Philadelphia that evening. About half of the Fabulous Fifty were going home, and since there wasn't a special train, it didn't make any difference when we left. "What do you think?" I asked Tony.

He looked at his new clothes unfolded on the bed. "Let's go home."

"Tell you what," Dan said. "There's an eight o'clock express with a diner. If you pack now, we can get you on it, and I'll call your folks and tell them to meet you at Broad Street Station." We gave him our telephone numbers and started packing. Between the things he had brought with him and the new clothes, Tony had some overflow and I put it in my bag. I wore my blue suit, and we both wore wristwatches. It only took a few minutes to pack. We met Harry Johnson in the lobby saying good-bye to some of the other winners. "Now don't forget, we have some more premiums, and we'll see that you get them at home," he was saying as we walked up. He turned to us with a smile. "Well, boys, I see you're leaving us too. Did you have a good time?"

"It was great," Tony said. "Really great."

"The best treat of my life." I really meant it.

Harry beamed. "We didn't expect to have anyone your age on this trip, and I must say it's been a pleasure to have you along. Both of you." He winked at me and we shook hands. "Have a good ride home."

Tiny was right behind us when we turned around. "C'mon, I'll take your bags out. I guess you guys had a good trip, huh?"

"I'll say. How did you make out on the Series?"

"Not so bad. I made a hundred bucks on the games and another hundred in tips." He leaned closer and whispered, "And I had a great one with a doll from Nashville. She was here with her old man. That was the best play of the Series." He made an *okay* sign. "Come back and see us, right?"

"We will. Thanks for the tips and have a good year, Tiny." He put the bags in the cab and without talking about it we each tipped him a dollar. It was instinct. After all, I thought, he got us started.

At Pennsylvania Station I felt like an old-timer. A redcap took our bags down to the platform and put them aboard the parlor car—a last splurge by the *Clarion*. I looked at my watch. "We still have ten minutes before the train leaves. C'mon with me."

"Where we goin'?"

"To look at the engine." Sure enough, it was a K4, number 2445, not as new or shiny as number 3775 that had pulled our special train. It still had the same good smells and noises as the other one. The driving wheels towered over us and the polished connecting rods gleamed in the platform lights. "It's really big, ain't it?" Tony said.

"Yep, it's a K-Four Pacific. Those are eighty-inch drivers."

"I didn't know you knew that stuff."

"You know what color it is?"

"It looks black to me."

"Not when it's washed. It's Brunswick green."

"Green, huh?" I could tell he was impressed. We walked back toward the tender. I was hoping that Abby would be in the cab, but this engineer was thin and wore glasses. "Hi," I called up to him.

"Hello there, boys. You riding with us?"

"Yes, sir. When was your K4 built?"

"1917. She's just a baby."

"At Altoona?"

"No, Juniata. Sounds like you know something about engines. Want to come up?"

I looked down at my new suit. "I better not today, but thank you. Would you blow off some steam for my friend, please?"

The engineer leaned into the cab and looked at a gauge. "What do we have, Al?" He leaned out again. "She's going to do that herself in a minute. I'll clean the cylinder cocks for you, though."

"What are the cyl—Yow!!" Tony jumped when the steam shot out on the platform. He was just as scared as I had been. "Boy, I thought somethin' was wrong."

I waved up to the engineer. "Thanks a lot."

"You're welcome. Have a good ride."

We walked back to the parlor car. The porter was standing at the door. "Understand you gentlemen are planning to have dinner. Why don't you go right up to the diner now and get yourself a good table?"

"Thank you, that's a good idea."

There were only a few other people in the diner, but it filled up as soon as the train started moving. It felt a lot different coming home from New York than it had going. "That was a good start," I said as we accelerated smoothly out of the station. "I like the way he handles his cutoff."

Tony looked at me as if I was talking a foreign language, and then looked back at the menu. "What are you going to eat?"

He ordered a steak and I had French lamb chops. I guessed they called them French because they had frilly little paper cuffs over the ends of the bones. It felt great eating on the train. I tried to see lights outside, but mostly everything was reflected back from the inside of the car. There was white linen on the tables and nice china and glasses, and silver covers over the serving dishes like at the Plaza. The waiters carried the food up and down the aisles without even noticing the motion of the car. When we came up on the Jersey side, the train began to speed up and the locomotive whistle wailed back to us: Dah-dah-dit-daahh. "Level crossing," I said.

Tony looked up from his steak. "You're such a big-mouth, greaseball, you know that?"

When we were ordering dessert, Sam Hart and Jim Hilferty came into the dining car. "Well, hi there!" Sam said. "We didn't know you were on the train."

"We're in the parlor car."

"Pretty fancy. We just have regular Pullman tickets. Well, I could tell that Harry liked you two. We just made it at the last minute. Jim called Alice and got homesick."

"You'll understand when you're married," Jim said. "It's been fun having you along. You call me if you ever need anything out West Philly way, okay?"

"Like a Cadillac," Sam said. "Same here. You'll be buying a house one of these days, and I'll get you a good deal." They gave us their cards, and we wrote our names and addresses in their notebooks. "Thanks, boys, you have a good ride home. We better get some dinner before we're in Philadelphia."

They walked up to an empty table, and Tony and I ordered dessert: pumpkin pie with sherry sauce for him and hot apple pie with vanilla sauce for me. The waiter showed Tony how to prick his pie with a fork and pour the sauce over it. "First pumpkin of the season, nice and fresh," he said with a dazzling smile.

After dinner we went back to our seats. The few lights that whizzed past outside looked blurred and mysterious. The car rocked gently from side to side as the rails clicked under our wheels. Every thirty-nine feet, Sam said; they made them that long so they would fit in a forty-foot gondola car. I felt relaxed and contented. "North Philadelphia!" the conductor called as he passed through the car. The train began to slow down and a few people stood in the aisle and gathered their things together. Tony and I sat up and watched out the window as we stopped. North Philadelphia Station looked small, cold, and dimly lit. Most of the people meeting the train were wearing overcoats. We saw Sam Hart puff along the platform carrying his suitcase, and then a plump lady came up and hugged him. "There go Morello's buddies," Tony said. The two men who had sat across from us at the banquet were walking toward the stairs with a couple of short, black-coated women. Three boys in knickers followed behind carrying their bags. We couldn't hear them talking; it was like watching a movie. The train began to move again. "I'll get you gentlemen's bags ready in the vestibule," the porter said. "Your folks meetin' you?"

"I think so."

"We'll have a redcap take these right up to your auto."

I sort of nodded; I didn't want to tell him that we didn't have an auto.

The conductor came through the car again. "Suburban Station—Broad Street," he called. In a minute we were sliding past the platforms. There were many more people than at North Philadelphia, but it was hard to recognize anyone while we were moving. Then the brakes hissed, and we came to a stop. I tipped the porter a quarter; it had become second nature in two weeks. "Thank you, sir. You young gentlemen have a good year." He had already passed our bags to a redcap who followed us down the platform as we looked for our folks.

Sometimes whether you see somebody or not depends on whether you recognize them. I saw my mother and father and Elena and Georgios long before they saw us. They were standing with Tony's parents, another lady, and a heavyset man in an overcoat with his back to us. They seemed to be looking right at us and I waved, but they didn't notice. I waved again; no luck. Finally we walked right up next to the heavy man and I said, "Mom, Dad!" They both jumped. My mother held out her arms to me and then stopped. "Hey, don't I get a hug?"

She gave me a little hug, not like home at all. My father looked at me as if I were a ghost. "Poppa." He held out his hand hesitantly, and we shook. Elena smiled and hugged me, and Georgios just stared. Tony's mom was crying and hugging him as if she would never let him go. "Take it easy, Luisa, you'll break him," the heavy man said. This time I jumped: It was Morello. He was holding hands with the other woman. "This is my wife, Maria. This is Sol Janus, the kid I told you about."

"How do you do, ma'am," I said.

She smiled shyly up at me. *"Bello,"* she said.

"Sì, bello," Mrs. Ammanati said, and smiled at me too. My mother was looking at my clothes and the suitcase and the bag that said Fabulous Fifty.

"Let's get outa here," Morello said to Tony and me. "I called ahead and got us a couple of cars." We followed him up the stairs and the parents walked behind. There were two Lincoln sedans parked at the curb, and my parents stared when Tony and I each tipped the redcap a quarter. He touched his hat and smiled. "Thank you, gentlemen."

"You're welcome," I said. My father looked at me again. "Just tell the driver where you want to go," Morello said. "And if you need anything taken care of, give me a call."

"Thank you." It felt funny shaking hands with him.

"No hard feelings?"

"No hard feelings."

"I'll call you after school tomorrow," Tony said.

We each rode home with our own families, and I sat up front with the driver and gave him directions. My folks didn't say anything, and when Georgios started to ask me questions my father told him to be quiet. He tried to pick up both suitcases when the driver dropped us off, and I let him carry the canvas one into the house.

Everything looked different: smaller and shabbier. I had

never been away from home before, and I wondered if Paul and Robert felt like this when they came home from camp. My mother took off her coat and came over and felt the lapel of my suit. *"Oraios,"* she said, shaking her head. I opened the suitcase and took out the gift-boxed tie for my father, the scarves, and the pocketknife. I gave my mom her scarf first and watched her open the box and unfold the tissue paper delicately. "Oh, *Oraios!*" Rine had helped me pick it out; it was a paisley pattern with purple and gold and blues and oranges; I thought she could wear it for Easter. She held it against her dress, and then she came over and took my face between her hands and kissed me. *"Efkharisto para poli!"* I was glad she liked it so much; it was the most colorful thing she owned. Elena's was even brighter, and she was just as thrilled.

I told my dad to open his box next. The tie I had picked out for him was dark blue like his, but instead of white dots it had little white diamonds with light blue centers. It reminded me of the Greek flag. He took it out, felt the silk, and made the same expression as when he handled a good piece of hardware. Rine had left the small square price tag that said, "Pure Silk, $2" on the back. My father was shocked. He squinted at the price closely. "Too much," he said disapprovingly, "too much."

"My present," I said.

"Efkharisto." He had no choice. Anything else would have been bad manners.

Georgios was hopping up and down with excitement. I made him close his eyes and put the little red box in his hand. He opened it carefully. It was a small penknife in a leather case. It had engraved nickel-silver sides, a pen blade, a nail file, and a tiny scissors. "That's for when you grow up and become a gentleman."

He threw his arms around my neck. "Thank you, thank you, thank you! My first knife!"

"Only for good," my father said. "Not for every day." He held out his hand for it and looked it over carefully. "All this you won?"

"This and more." I showed them the suitcase, the pants and sweater, the shirts and ties and underwear. My mother marveled at each thing. Then I showed them the prizes from the Fabulous Fifty bag. "The other club members get first choice of these, but I'm sure there will be some left. There are more coming too, because they didn't have all the premiums in New York. Here's the picture that they took of us on the roof of the *Clarion* building."

"I want to see you," Georgios said.

I pointed to Tony and me. "There we are. The Fabulous Fifty-One."

"And those dummies never even knew?"

"Not then, at the beginning."

"How much you won?" my father asked.

"A hundred and seventy dollars. Plus the fifteen we made from tickets. I have fifty dollars left."

"And lost?"

"Nothing."

"Is not good to bet so much money," my mother said in a low voice.

"If he wins, is good," my father said.

CHAPTER 34

I was so tired that I barely had time to think that my own bed felt strange before I fell asleep. I woke up to the alarm clock feeling like I could have slept through the whole day. It was cold and gray when I left for school wearing my new sweater; another Philadelphia winter was on the way.

School was amazing, everyone seemed to know where I had been. Boys I didn't know, upperclassmen, came up and shook my hand and asked how it was. It turned out that the roof picture had been published in the *Clarion* and so had many others of our group, including the one of Tony and Babe Ruth. Of course there was a message in my homeroom telling me to report to Dr. Farnsworth's office. I had a note for him from my parents, another one from Harry Johnson, and I was as well prepared as a trial lawyer.

It turned out I didn't need any of it. When I walked in, Dr. Farnsworth was looking through some papers with a stern expression on his face. He turned to me. "Well, what do you have to say for yourself?"

"I had a wonderful time, sir."

"You realize that you've missed two weeks of work in every class?"

"Yes, sir, but I'll make it up. It was the best trip of my life."

"Tell me about it."

I started from the beginning and told him the whole story. When I got to the part about Mr. Leonard leaving, he interrupted me. "So you thought you'd just stay on in his place."

"Yes, sir. And by that time we knew that Harry Johnson wanted me to. I thought, *Carpe diem,* sir."

"*Carpe diem* indeed, Janus. Very good."

It took an hour to tell about the trip and I still left a lot out. At the end he smiled and said, "I envy you, Janus. But I expect you to make up every scrap of work."

"I will, sir. I promise." He never even asked for my notes.

After school I took my new pants to a Ukrainian tailor on Third Street to have them cuffed. He turned them inside out and inspected them, making clicking noises with his tongue. "Nice goods you got," he said. "Not local."

"No, I got them in New York."

"Nice goods," he said again. I put them on, and he got down on the floor and pinned the cuffs. "I can have tomorrow."

"Really?" I looked at the big pile of clothes on the table next to his sewing machine. He waved them away. "Local. Not goods like this."

"Tony called you," my mom said when I came in.

"*Efkharisto,* Momma." I gave her a hug, and she held on tight. She felt smaller than I remembered. "The school—?" she began.

"It's fine, Momma. The principal wanted to hear all about the trip. I have some work to make up, that's all." I called Tony back, and he said that the *Clarion* had sent over another box of premiums for each of us. "There's some neat stuff," he said. "Another wallet, a leather diary, a *World Almanac*—"

"Let's give them to those guys tonight. We can have a special meeting."

"Great, I'll call everybody. What'd your old man say?"

"About what?"

"About playing hooky, everything."

"Nothing. I can't figure it out."

"I told you, sport, money talks. I'll see you tonight."

"How about if I help carry the stuff? I'll come over to your house first."

At quarter to seven Tony and I left for Harry's house, each carrying a Fabulous Fifty bag in one hand and balancing a carton on the other shoulder. "This stuff weighs a ton," Tony complained.

"We don't have far to go."

"There's one thing in here I forgot to tell you about."

"What's that?"

"You'll see. It's the best prize of all." After all the great prizes we had been given, I wondered what Tony thought was the best.

Mrs. Goodman opened the door for us, and when we walked in, the other guys shouted, "Yaayy, Tony! Yaayy, Sol!" There were bottles of soda and big bowls of pretzels and potato chips on the kitchen table. We gave the club handshake all around, and the other guys clapped us on the back. "How was it? We want to hear everything," Mark said.

"That'll take a week. How about if you guys get some prizes first." I could tell that Bobby could hardly wait to see what was making the Fabulous Fifty bags bulge. "Was there really a camera like they said in the paper?" he asked.

Tony opened his bag and took out the Kodak and the rolls of film. "Gosh," Bobby said, "I never believed they would really give away anything like that." Then I opened mine and put the second camera next to Tony's. "Two!" Bobby said, his eyes wide. "You got two cameras!"

"Sure, we got two of everything."

"I never thought of that," Harry said. "We didn't know what to think when you didn't come home."

"Neither did we for a while." I took out the picture. "Here we are on the roof of the *Clarion* building. The Fabulous Fifty-One."

"I have that picture," Harry said. "I saved everything from the newspapers."

"The Fabulous Fifty-One," Mark repeated. "What a bunch of dopes, they never even caught on."

"Yes they did," I said. "Some of them, anyway. It's a long story."

"I want to hear the whole thing," Harry said. He opened bottles of soda for all of us. "Here's to the Fabulous Fifty-One."

"Right! We did it!" Bobby cheered.

It took two hours to distribute the presents. The other three were going to choose up to see who went first, but Harry said, "We don't need to do that, let's just go by the alphabet. I don't mind Bobby going first."

"Okay with me," Mark said.

They went around and around, and once the cameras and the field glasses and the first three pocketknives had been chosen they made Tony and me join in. "Anything there's more than three of, it's only right," Mark said. "You guys brought the stuff home." The one thing I really wanted was a wristwatch, and when Harry chose one of the pocket watches I knew I would get one. "I always wanted one like the rich guys wear on those chains across their vest," he said.

When we finished, there were big piles in front of Bobby, Harry, and Mark. Bobby kept picking up his camera, his watch, and his pen-and-pencil set. "It's all brand-new," he said three or four times. I kept a watch, the *Clarion* picture, two mechanical pencils that I could use in school, and the *World Almanac* because nobody else wanted it.

"Now look at this," Tony said. He reached into the carton and took out the last thing, a small square box sealed with paper tape. "How come it doesn't say what it is?" Bob asked.

"So nobody would swipe it." Tony slit the tape, opened the box carefully, and lifted out a tissue-wrapped sphere. He unwrapped it and held it out in his hand. It was an official baseball covered with signatures. "Every player on both teams," he said. "Even Babe Ruth."

"Honest?" Mark said. "Babe Ruth?"

Tony pointed to the Babe's autograph. "Just like the one on my program."

I was surprised by his reverence. I guessed he really meant it when he said he wanted to be a baseball player. "Well, who wants it?" You could see that it hurt him to ask.

"I pass," Bobby said. "It would just get beat up at my house."

Harry scratched his ear. "Well, there are two of them, right? I'd sort of like it. Let me think about it."

"I'd really like it," Mark said. Tony's face fell. "Here it

is," he said, and handed it carefully to Mark.

"Gee, thanks, Tony. This is worth everything."

"Your turn," Tony said to me.

I still had two boxes in my carton. "Hey, Harry," I said, "I forgot something." I held up the second pocket watch that no one had taken. "Would you like this better?"

His face lit up. "Two pocket watches! I'd be like a bank president!"

"One for each eye," Mark said, and we all laughed. I handed Harry the box.

"Well, I guess that wraps it up," Tony said. He put his carton on the floor.

"Hey, Tony," I said. He looked up. "Catch." I tossed him the other autographed ball.

"You mean it?"

"It's yours."

"Boy, thanks, greaseball. You're the best vice president any club ever had."

When I got home, I found Elena working on a scrapbook. It turned out that she had saved all the newspaper pictures and articles too. I gave her the game programs, the banquet menu, and the other papers I had brought home. My mother sat next to her, looking at the pictures like they were from another world.

I didn't want to take off my Elgin watch when I went to bed that night. I read the instructions carefully—they said to always wind it in the morning, never at night. They also said that it had seven real jewels inside. I resisted the temptation to open the back cover and look. I slept ten hours straight.

Saturday morning after breakfast I called Paul Fraser.

We talked for half an hour, and he invited me to dinner Sunday night. I guess I should have worked in the store, but I felt restless. I put on my new sweater and walked over to the tailor shop and sure enough my pants were on the pressing board. "Only a minute," the tailor said. He charged me a dollar, and I could tell when I paid him that it was a top price. I pulled the curtain on his little alcove and changed into them right there.

I started to walk home, and when I turned the corner of South Street there was Tony sitting on Old Man Casati's steps reading Casati's Saturday morning *Clarion*. He was wearing long pants too. The steps were cold, but not like at the end of winter, and my new wool pants were warmer than corduroy knickers. "Hi, sport. I stopped over your house but you were out," he said. He turned the paper back from the sports section to the front page. There was a small row of stars above a column headline: FABULOUS FIFTY RETURN IN TRIUMPH—CONTEST A HUGE SUCCESS. "How about that?" Tony said. I read through the article and then we looked at each other. Tony poked an elbow in my ribs. "See, I told ya, you dumb Greek."

TEAM MEMBERS IN THE 1921 WORLD SERIES

New York Giants (National League)

Dave Bancroft, shortstop
Jesse Barnes, pitcher
George Burns, center field
Phil Douglas, pitcher
Frank Frisch, third base
George Kelly, first base
Irish Meusel, left field

Art Nehf, pitcher
John Rawlings, second base
Earl Smith, catcher
Frank Snyder, catcher
Fred Toney, pitcher
Ross Youngs, right field

New York Yankees (American League)

Frank Baker, third base
Rip Collins, pitcher
Al DeVormer, catcher
Chick Fewster, left field
Harry Harper, pitcher
Waite Hoyt, pitcher
Carl Mays, pitcher
Mike McNally, third base
Bob Meusel, right field
Elmer Miller, center field

Roger Peckinpaugh, short-stop
Bill Piercey, pitcher
Wally Pipp, first base
Jack Quinn, pitcher
Tom Rogers, pitcher
Babe Ruth, left field
Wally Schang, catcher
Bob Shawkey, pitcher
Aaron Ward, second base

3